MW01182039

The Way We Were:
Adventures in Childhood
by
Creative Quills Writing Group

Creative Quills Publishing Group
El Reno, OK

ISBN: 13:978-0998643625

This book goes out to all parents,
biological & otherwise,
for bringing us into the world to create this mayhem!

Some of these stories are true. Some are not.
Can you tell which are which?
If you can correctly identify the true stories and the fiction, you
may win a copy of our next book! Contact Andrea Foster at
Booklady@pldi.net with your guess!

Index

Preface

Whether too painful to remember, or too pleasant to forget, childhood memories waft through our gray matter like cumulus clouds in a classic climate.

Join our authors in this book by reliving both fact and fiction, folly and frolic, joy and jest, and the pure fun of childhood nostalgia.

To paraphrase the author of wisdom, "Unless you become as a little child, you can in no wise inherit the Kingdom of Heaven." Welcome to and please enjoy *The Way We Were: Adventures in Childhood.*

--Chuck Baker

Just Another Day On The Farm

Judy K. Bishop

Slowly, the large heavy barn door opened, rollers squeaking with each small movement. A wide open door revealed two young boys standing there looking into the old red barn as if trying to decide whether to go in or not. Sonny, ten years old, and Dylan, six years old, were cousins, looking for an adventure.

They loved visiting Grandma Alice and Grandpa Earl, because they lived on a small farm which offered unlimited opportunities of exploration and temptations for young, curious boys. Three barns, a small pond, twenty-seven acres, horses, chickens, barn cats, and trees to climb were just a taste of what the farm held on its menu.

Mitzi, an Australian Cattle Dog, loved to tag along with the boys and get involved in their adventures…and occasionally, trouble.

Mitzi had been a young stray that showed up on the farm five years ago and never left. When the boys weren't around, she was Grandpa Earl's constant companion while working on the farm.

Sonny and Dylan had built a fort in the farthest pasture on the farm and often hid out there from outlaws, drifters and Indians. They had scoured the fields for weeks in search of materials for their fort. Fallen tree limbs from the big shady oak trees, sections of discarded rusty wire fencing, rocks, and some metal fence posts had gone into creating their unique fort. Cleverly woven into the midst of a group of tangled bushes, the fort was well camouflaged.

Sonny's younger sister, Lila, was unaware the fort even existed, which was how they liked it. They didn't want girls in their fort anyway. She mostly stayed in the farmhouse with Grandma Alice and made cookies or did some other girly activity.

On this particular day, the boys were bored with the fort and looking for something new to capture their attention. They had wandered through two of the old barns before heading to the big red barn hoping to find something interesting to do in there.

Standing in the open barn door, they gazed around and saw the horse bridles hanging on the stall doors, a shelf with horse brushes, just the usual stuff that was always there. They weren't supposed to play in this barn, but that rule seemed to have slipped their minds at this particular moment. It was long and narrow with horse stalls down one side and a dirt floor perfect for anyone boarding horses to ride indoors during bad weather.

They started walking down the long narrow dirt floor, looking around as they went. Then something unusual caught Sonny's attention. There sat Grandpa Earl's golf cart, not locked away in a stall as usual...with the key in it.

Sonny immediately went into action and jumped up on the seat. "Let's drive it back to the fort!"

Dylan wasn't so quick to join in. "Grandpa will get mad. Let's just walk back to the fort."

"No, this will be fun," said Sonny, his deep blue eyes sparkling, already enticed by the scent of a new adventure. "We won't stay long, and Grandpa will never know. He isn't home right now anyway."

Dylan was getting more nervous as Sonny kept insisting they take the golf cart for a little spin. "We don't know how to drive it anyway, so let's just go."

"I know how to drive! I've ridden with Grandpa lots of times and watched him. It's easy! Get in."

Sonny was certainly the more rascally of the two, and the cowlick in his blonde unruly hair added to his daring demeanor. Dylan, less daring, could easily be misled into following Sonny, his idol, in his escapades.

"I'm going in and tell Grandma."

"You sissy! It will be fun! Don't you want to have fun? And you better not tell Grandma if you know what's good for you."

"But we might get in trouble. Let's just walk to the fort," pleaded Dylan.

"Get in, Dylan, or I am going without you."

Reluctantly, Dylan got in, Sonny confidently turned the key starting the electric golf cart, and they slowly headed toward the open barn door, picking up speed as they went.

Reaching the open door, they bolted out into the barnyard at high speed, the beginning of a daring mission with Dylan gripping the seat handle tightly as Sonny laughed, the wind blowing through his curly hair. Freedom!

They made the sharp turn outside the barn and

headed for the pasture gate, narrowly missing some chickens, with an excited Mitzi barking and running alongside.

Dylan screamed as two wheels slightly left the ground on the turn. The cart passed through the broken down pasture gate with Sonny driving full speed over the rough terrain and breaking out into the open field at last.

Dylan finally started to relax and enjoy the adventure, forgetting about Grandpa Earl. Passing under the large oak tree which marks the half way point to the fort, a black crow scolded them from his perch high in the tree. Horses in a nearby pasture briefly looked up from grazing upon hearing the squeals and laughter of the boys.

"Sonny, you really do know how to drive! This is fun".

"I told you it's easy. Aren't you glad you came?"

They reached the fort, Sonny slammed on the brakes, and they skidded sideways to a halt. Checking out the fort, they found some damage which must have happened from the recent storm. After quickly doing repairs, they then sat down to rest and enjoy the sunny day.

Finally, Dylan spoke up, "Sonny, we better go back. Grandpa will be coming home."

"Ok, climb in." Off they went with the same fervor and speed that brought them there: back through the same path in the field, past the horses again, through the broken down pasture gate, and making the sharp turn to head back to the barn. Mitzi ran ahead knowing they were heading home.

Sonny aimed the cart in the direction of the barn

Door, and Dylan yelled, "Slow down! You're going too fast!" right before his side of the golf cart scraped against the doorway. Sonny reacted by turning the wheel sharply, causing the back fender to hit the wall as well. The scraping and crunching sounds echoed in the barn, and finally Sonny brought the cart to a halt.

Slowly getting out, not anxious to view the damage, the boys stood staring in disbelief at the long scrape down the side and the damaged back fender. Dylan began to cry, "You broke Grandpa's cart. He's going to be mad. We're in big trouble now, and it's all your fault. I told you we shouldn't do it."

Sonny didn't want Dylan to know, but he was scared too. Not only was Grandpa Earl going to be mad, but their parents would be furious.

Finally Sonny spoke, "Let's go back to the house. Maybe our parents will pick us up before Grandpa gets home, and maybe he won't notice it's broken right away and will think some stranger did it. And stop crying!" yelled Sonny, having no sympathy for Dylan.

Slowly, they headed up the sidewalk to the house and entered the back door which led to the heart of the farm house, the kitchen. Grandma and Lila had just finished making peanut butter cookies. The aroma of fresh baked cookies filled the kitchen and engulfed the boys as they entered, momentarily causing them to forget about their dire situation.

"Hi, boys! It's about time you came in. Your parents will be here any minute to pick you up," said Grandma Alice. "Have you boys been having fun?"

Dylan hung his head and didn't answer, but Sonny spoke up. "Yes, Grandma, we did. Can we have some cookies?"

Just then the phone rang. It was Dylan's dad, saying he would be picking up both boys, but later than planned. Grandma Alice passed along the information to the boys and was about to hang up when Sonny asked "How much later?"

"Brad, how much later will you be?" asked Grandma. "Ok, we'll see you then," and she hung up.

"What did he say, Grandma?"

"Just an hour later, dear, but now you will get to see Grandpa. He will be home in about fifteen minutes and will be so glad to see all of you children."

Sonny and Dylan looked at each other as fear began to creep across their faces. "Come on, Dylan, let's go watch TV." Sonny wanted to get out of the room as fast as possible before Dylan started crying again.

A few minutes later, they heard Grandpa Earl come in and greet Lila and Grandma Alice. "Where are the boys?" he said loudly as he waited for them to answer.

"We're in here watching TV, Grandpa," Sonny yelled from the living room. Dylan hadn't said a word since they came in.

"Well, come in here, and give your ole Grandpa a big hug."

Slowly, they entered the kitchen, went over to give Grandpa Earl a hug, then scurried back into the living room.

"They must be watching something extremely

interesting, the way they hurried back to the TV. How long before dinner is ready, Alice?"

"About thirty minutes."

"Well then, I think I will go on out to the barn and feed the horses."

Upon hearing this, Sonny and Dylan looked at each other, eyes wide with fear. Oh no, they were hoping to be heading home before Grandpa went to the barn. Sonny's heart began to beat faster, and tears welled up in Dylan's eyes again. Their goose was cooked for sure, now!

Fifteen minutes later, they heard the kitchen door open as Grandpa Earl and Ronnie, who had a horse boarded at the farm, entered.

"Earl, whatever is the matter? Your face is all red. Are you all right?" asked Grandma Alice. "Hi, Ronnie, good to see you."

"I'm fine, but there is a something I need to get to the bottom of. I was in the barn moving the golf cart out of the way, so Ronnie could ride his horse and saw that the cart is all banged up! Has anyone been back to the barn today?"

"No, Ronnie called to say he wouldn't be coming until late afternoon, and I saw him pulling in right before you walked in the door. No one else."

There was silence, the boys offering no explanation as they waited nervously to find out what would happen next. Maybe Grandpa would just let it go and not ask any questions. But that turned out to be too much to hope for.

"Boys, can you come in here please?" asked Grandpa Earl. They walked into the kitchen and could see the anger on his face. Oh no, here it comes.

"Boys, were you playing in the big barn today?"

Dylan hung his head, and Sonny took a deep breath before saying, "Well, we were in there for a little while."

"The golf cart is banged up. Do you know anything about that?"

Both boys were silent.

"Boys…I expect an answer…and the truth."

Sonny, even though mischievous, always told the truth and finally spoke up. "Well, we took it out for a little drive back to our fort."

"And do you know how it got damaged?"

"Well, uh, we were driving it back into the barn and came too close to the wall when we went through the barn door, and it scraped the side. When I turned the wheel to get away from the wall, the back fender hit the wall. I'm sorry, Grandpa. We didn't mean to tear it up."

"Dylan, were you with Sonny when this happened? Were you in the cart, too?"

Feebly, Dylan answered, "Yes."

Grandpa Earl was silent, and then Ronnie spoke up. "Earl, I've done a lot of repairs on my own cart, and I think I can fix it back good as new."

Grandpa Earl slowly turned around to Ronnie standing behind him. "I would appreciate that, Ronnie," and a small smile crossed his face as he shook his head side to side slightly before turning back to the boys.

"Boys, you're lucky Ronnie can fix the cart. I hope you know never to do anything like that again. You took the cart without me knowing, and besides, you could have been hurt."

Both boys looked up at Grandpa Earl, Dylan with his little innocent face, tears in his eyes, and Sonny, looking guilty, and said, "Sorry, Grandpa."

Then Sonny added, "We won't do it again."

Grandpa Earl and Ronnie turned, heading out the door to return to the barn. Once outside, Grandpa Earl turned to Ronnie and said, "Those boys, they remind me of things I did as a young boy, so how can I stay mad at them?"

"I know, I have grandsons of my own. You just wonder what they will do next, but you sure do love 'em anyway."

Freedom is Named Aunt Ouida

PJ Acker

Sun sparkling off glistening white strands of long hair, prematurely white, it free-floats above the steering wheel of a red Cadillac convertible. The mammoth metal giant barreling down the road toward you would be your first sign of my aunt's impending visit. Bright blue eyes, rosy cheeks and a huge smile in the windshield would be your next clue.

These events announced an impromptu visit from one of my favorite aunts. Their unexpectedness was the very thing that made them so wonderful. You just never knew when it might happen. Like a gift when it wasn't even Christmas or your birthday—a shiny box with a great, wonderful bow just shows up one morning in the middle of your average, routine day.

It's absolutely the best kind of surprise!

My aunt is a free-spirit, you see. And to my understanding, isn't much concerned or bothered by other people's rules or opinions, which is another thing that makes her quite one of the most intriguing and marvelous human beings I've ever met.

After the Cadillac that caught a little air topping the hill slows and stops in your driveway, a cloud of joyous laughter drifts out as the massive car door opens, and before you know it, you're enveloped in a world-class hug. Oh yes, my aunt is quite one of the best huggers EVER. A warmer, more loving and joyous soul I don't think exists.

My father's little sister, my Aunt Ouida is truly a delight and is absolutely the female version of my father. They have the same expressive, charmingly mischievous grins that fully reaches beautiful blue eyes that twinkle with unsuppressed mirth.

What makes her so enchanting is not just her smile, her conversation is sprinkled with giggles and punctuated with titters of joy—quite infectious actually. One would have to be absolutely determined to be miserable to remain in a bad humor in her presence for any reasonable length of time.

She is married to a loving husband as far as I could see, who, after he retired, developed what some might call an "adventurous streak." A pilot with his own plane, his renewed interest in fishing and hunting had him quite literally "flying off into the sunset" to pursue said interests frequently, leaving my aunt to her own devices.

This might have been a problem for some women, but not my aunt. Thus was born what I think of as my aunts "traveling era."

Our family is a large clan, and my aunt always was a very social person, to begin with. Her journeys began with visiting relatives scattered over the state and surrounding areas. These visits were often unexpected and spur-of-the-moment, which made them all the more magical...at least, to me.

With a girlfriend or cousin in tow but often solo, my aunt would jump into her car and off she would go, calling to announce her imminent arrival to the object of her visit while she was en route...sometimes. Very exciting to a twelve year old!

Of course, with this particular mode of operation, one would have to be flexible and prepared with a list of several potential alternatives. This never seemed a problem, as her visits were always short, thoroughly entertaining, and were always looked forward to by all. But, if the odd thing happened and no one was at home, there were plenty of museums, IMAX theaters and sites to see until the next person on the visiting list could be reached.

My aunt taught me the value of taking responsibility for your own happiness, knowing how to entertain yourself, and how not to sit around and complain. She was a living example of how to seek out your own joy and how not to pout, whine and feel sorry for yourself, because that basically takes time away from the time you'll have for your next new adventure!

Memories of my First 4th of July

Rosemarie Durgin

The year was 1945. I was six years old. Mother and I were living in Bamberg, in northern Bavaria, in western Germany, in the American Sector.

We had arrived there a few months previously, just before the end of the war. During most of the last year of that war, my mother and I had lived in the Bohemian Forest to get away from the constant bombings. Once the Czech people had reclaimed their country, they evicted us, the hated German invaders, Mother and I amongst them.

We had spent a week on a train for the approximately fifty-mile trip back into Germany. Mother and I were among many people who left Cheb in a cattle car that day. We chose to stay on that train for as long as possible. Why she wanted to go to Bamberg, I don't know, perhaps because that was the town that was the furthest from the border, or because she had hoped to meet some friends there, who might be able to help her. She always claimed that we had been lucky indeed, for winding up in the American Sector.

Mother and I were alone in Bamberg. She did not have many skills she could parley into a paying job. My father was missing in action somewhere on the Russian front. We did not know if any of our relatives had survived the war still raging in parts of the world.

Both of my parents were originally from Essen. We

knew that town had been the subject of frequent and devastating Allied bombings. We did not know if any one of our relatives had survived. Mail service was unreliable, if at all working at the time. So, my mother and I were alone without knowledge of any of our relatives.

Housing was impossible to obtain in Germany, for much housing had been lost to the bombings. Also, the thousands of refugees who had left their homes in the eastern provinces of the Great German Reich were searching for homes, for any place where they might live. For a few weeks, we shared very cramped quarters with some acquaintances, Mother sleeping on a couch and me on a pallet on the floor.

But mother persevered, and after some time she found us a room all to ourselves. We were so fortunate to find a private room for us alone. It was an attic room on the fourth floor of an apartment house. There was no heat, and there was no water. We shared the toilet with two other families who lived on the third floor, but that was our room! Mother was able to find a small potbellied stove to heat our haven and to cook our meals. We shared the bed, and we had a small table and two chairs, and a wardrobe held all our belongings, but the room was ours alone. We were so grateful, so blessed.

The best thing about the room was the window. I could look out over the red tile roofs of town. I saw all the churches and even the Altenburg castle up on its hill. The building we lived in was one of the tallest structures on our street. Across from us were mostly farmhouses of one story in height. I could listen to the church bells as they tolled the hours and called the worshipers to services. Best of all, I could watch for my mother as she rounded the corner onto our street on her way home from work late every evening. Mother had found employment at the Red Cross American Service Men's Club, a little snack bar for the American service men stationed in Bamberg. She did not make much money, but the little she earned kept us fed and paid the rent for our little room.

I remember this particular day very well. It was summer time and stayed light outside for a long time. Mother usually arrived from work at about dusk. For some unfathomable reason, she was late that day. And then the bombings started! I could hear the explosions. Toward the center of town, right by the bridge that Mother had to cross, the flack was responding. I could see the explosions. The entire sky was lighted red and green and white. Smoke was rising above the river several blocks away.

Night was falling, and Mother still was not home. What was keeping her? Soon, it was pitch dark, and I could no longer see the alley where she was to turn into our street. Was the bridge she had to cross bombed out? Had Mother been on that bridge when the bombs had hit it? Would I ever see my mother again? I was petrified. And the explosions did not stop. On and on they went. How was I to survive without my mother? I could not stop the tears. Fear had me shaking, trembling. Still, the detonations continued and the flares lightened the sky un-abated. Who would take me in? We knew so few people in Bamberg, none of them able to keep another child.

I kept looking out of that window, and still my

mother did not come. Tears were streaming down my face. Where could I hide? Where was the nearest bomb shelter? I did not know. And the detonations continued. The sky was emblazoned with the colors of destruction. What were they bombing? It only happened in the direction of the bridge over the Regnitz. Finally, I crawled under our bed and covered my head with my pillow. I protected myself as well as I could manage from possible debris and promptly fell asleep.

That is how my mother found me when she returned home long after midnight. She explained that the Americans were celebrating some sort of holiday by shooting off fireworks. No bombs had been dropped on Bamberg. The bridge she had to cross to get home, had been blocked off, for that was the place from which the fireworks had been shot off. Mother explained that the Americans were shooting off colorful fireworks. The sounds I had heard were the fireworks, not bombs, and they were what caused the colorful lights in the sky over the river. They had been beautiful from her vantage point, she told me.

I could not imagine a celebration with fireworks. Mother tried to explain, but to a six-year-old, who knew only war and bombings, that made no sense whatsoever. Many years later, as I was working for the Americans, I finally realized I had witnessed the Fourth of July celebrations on the American Independence Day, that frightful evening of July the 4th, 1945.

Today as I watch the fireworks on Independence Day with pleasure, I think about that frightful day so long ago. Gone are the fears of my childhood. You see, I am now a naturalized citizen of this great country and have been for about fifty years, but I will never forget that first experience.

Day In The Park

Kandy Anderson

Slides, they twirl and whip around

But always lead you to the ground.

Teeters that totter push you up

It takes two, so you don't get stuck.

Have you tried the merry-go-round?

You must run fast, but don't fall down.

Let's play in the sand, or just sit and swing

And we can enjoy a cone of ice cream.

The best part of my day in the park

Would have to be sharing it...well before dark.

No Ordinary Pair of Shoes

Carol Nichols

Someone said, peace within makes beauty without. But I learned at an early age that fancy footwear goes a long way to making your outside appearance feel beautiful, even if it is only apparent to you.

My mother and my best friend Linda, along with her mother Alberta Chambers, took Linda and me to get shoes. It was in Downtown El Reno at the *Buster Brown* shoe store. We got to stand on this machine that looked more like a weight scale than a foot sizer, but it let us see our feet x-rayed.

We were then ushered to the back of the store to the children's area, and the shoes were brought out. What an array! Box after box was opened. Linda and I both were unimpressed as we sat, arms crossed and sporting big pouty faces.

The gentleman excused himself as he said, "Let's try one more box." He exited through the curtains from the back room with two of the biggest boxes I had ever seen. I remember thinking, "Those will surely be too big for me." Then the lid was opened, the tissue pulled back, and the white majorette boots were revealed.

They took my breath away, and as I bolted from my seat to touch and hold the pair, my mother quickly reseated me. I wanted to say, "Hurry up, shoe man, and get those fancy boots on my feet!" noting the look on Mother's face. I let the gentleman continue unwrapping each boot and placing them just out of my reach as he did the same for Linda.

I don't know if it was my exuberance toward the boots, but I was not the first in line any longer as Linda proudly marched up and down in front of the mirror that showcased the newest love of my life. But being in the second grade, I'm confident this was the only love of my life at that moment.

It finally came my turn, and I gleefully jumped from my chair and marched, in step, behind Linda. I remember thinking that mine were whiter. That gives me a chuckle, now…

Mother said, "Well, what do you think? Would you wear these?" and before I could answer, the salesman said, "Wait one minute, ladies," as he reached down and removed the paper from the top front of the boots revealing pristine white tassels. Our joy immediately escalated as Linda and I embraced and simultaneously jumped up and down. Could those boots have gotten any prettier? I think not.

We were allowed to wear them from the store, and I can remember Linda and me sitting in the back seat of that big old car, holding hands, with our feet extended, because the seats were so large, the bends of our knees didn't reach the edge of the seat.

Day after day, Linda and I proudly met at the corner of Macomb and Cooney to march, hand in hand, the two blocks to Central School, and I'm certain we were the toast of the playground.

Until I was asked to contribute to this endeavor, I never realized that my passion for footwear started at such an early age.

The Trench Coat

Alicia Ballard

I remember the man in the trench coat, the man that was both a phantom and a physical being. They would say that he would steal away children in the night, children who were bad. In a sense, he was like Krampus, except he was very real and very dangerous. He had killed between fifteen and thirty children before disappearing without a trace.

I was only ten years old when the first whispers of the man in the trench coat carried on the winds about the town. Four children had gone missing; search parties with dogs and policemen ran almost every night, until, one night, old Mr. Neil that lived down by the river claimed to have seen a man in a black trench coat with ruby buttons, throwing a small package into the river behind his house. He claimed his old sheep dog Mini was barking, and he had gone outside to quiet her.

"I thought them coons were back in 'the chicki' seed again!" proclaimed Mr. Neil.

A search party promptly was called and went to the river, fishing out the package Mr. Neil had described. Upon opening the sopping plastic, the police found the dismembered remains of my little brother. I remember the funeral in pieces, a rose on the casket and my mother crying. What I remember more clearly, however, is my time with my brother. The way he would laugh, the way we would play pirates or build a rocket ship out of cardboard boxes and take it to the moon.

*　　*　　*

The coffee shop was across the street from Lilian's bookstore. Business was slow today, so she decided to grab a cup of coffee to help her through her reorder list. A slim handsome man sat adjacent to the counter behind a tablet wirelessly attached to a rubber keyboard. He sipped an iced coffee as he looked at her, twice her age, yet butterflies erupted in her stomach under his gaze. She broke eye contact and ordered, choosing a table on the other side of the lobby.

Lilian read over her inventory list as she waited for her name to be called. A hand on her shoulder made her jump. She whipped her head around to see the slim man standing beside her.

"Sorry, I didn't mean to frighten you. You own the book store across the street, right?"

"Yes."

He smiled. "Then you know my cousin, Astrid. She talks about you all the time. My mother, her aunt, practically raised her."

Lilian felt relieved that this stranger hadn't come over to flirt with her but to greet someone he had heard about.

"Yes, she's my best friend. Practically my sister, your mother is a very kind woman."

"Thank you."

He smiled, but it didn't seem to reach his cool grey eyes. They held no warmth, and that caused chills to surge down Lilian's spine.

"Lilian!" the barista called.

"Oh, that's me. It was nice meeting you but I have to get back to the shop. Mittens, my cat, is the only one holding down the fort."

He laughed.

"He can only recommend the best books to sleep on."

"It was nice meeting you," he said and they parted ways.

*   *   *

Upon entering the shop, a sharp clang sounded from the back.

"Mittens!" Lilian called. She set down her coffee behind the counter. A knocking came from the back room, so soft she thought it might just be her imagination.

"Help!" The cry was so loud, it caused her to jump, nearly falling on her backside. The cry sounded like it came from a child.

"I'm coming!"

She ran to the back office, flinging the door open only to be greeted by Mitten's tired and confused meows.

"Hello?" Mittens cried at her in response, angry at being awoken from his nap.

"Sorry, buddy, I guess I'm just being paranoid."

Mitten's paws hit the floor with a plink as he dashed out of the office and into the bookshop.

"Mitt-" A sharp pain in the back of her head cut off her words. The glinting of a silver button was the last thing Lilian saw before her vision went black.

*　　*　　*

Her hands and feet were tightly bound, a tight cloth cutting into her cheeks and keeping her screams inside her mouth. A tall man in a billowing black trench coat stood over her, a long skinny blade in his pale hands. Lilian, suddenly a child again, felt the man to be too tall. She could not even see his face; he seemed to be as tall as a house.

"Little one, don't cry," he cooed. His voice only made more fresh tears gush from her eyes. She sucked in breath, her chest aching. The cloth made it difficult to get a good breath.

"It will be all right, it will only hurt for a second." He raised the blade up to her throat. She screamed in spite of the gag, wailing for her mother through the cloth.

"Shh," he whispered and caressed her face with his other hand. The blade pressed into her soft skin, cold and stinging. She could see his face now, the man from the coffee shop. His gray eyes cold and dead. A wretched smile cut into his face, making him look as if he were wearing a mask rather than his own skin. "Time to join your brother."

Lilian's eyes opened suddenly; it was all a dream. Yet, she was in an unfamiliar basement. She stood, head pounding. "Ugh."

She walked toward the staircase, only for her feet to be knocked out from under her. She hit the cement floor and rolled onto her side gasping to catch her breath. Once Lilian could breathe, she looked at her feet, only to find them chained to the wall. Hot tears burst from her eyes as she lay there, hopeless.

In a dark corner of the room, she noticed a small figure standing there, watching her. Her blood ran cold. The figure, having been noticed, moved forward. Its skin was blue and clammy, almost seeming loose on its bones. It shambled to her, barely holding itself up on its own two feet.

In horror, Lilian realized it was a child. "Oh my!" She was frozen in fear for a moment. "Sweetie," she croaked out at last. "How long have you been here? Did that man take you?"

"The man in the trench coat," the little boy replied, his voice watery as if it had been submerged in water for a long period of time. "He took me; he hurt me." His face was still obstructed by the shadows.

"I know, we'll get out of here. We'll get you back to your parents."

He pointed to his left. "There is only one way."

She looked, a small glint in the dark. She crawled over to find a broken glass bottle. "What am I going to do with this?"

The little boy didn't reply, only walked forward. His face came into the light, and Lilian bit hard against a scream. It was her dead brother, his eyes cloudy and goopy, the mouth and lips blue, his hair still dripping with foul water. He nodded and then was suddenly gone.

*   *   *

Lilian fell asleep, clutching the bottle's neck in her hand. The thump of the basement door closing woke her up.

"Hello," the man said in a sing-song voice. His boots made small tap-taps as he descended the stairs.

"Please," she cried, crawling on her knees. "I'll do anything." He came to her, a long skinny blade in his hand.

"Yes, you will." He placed the blade on a high shelf on the other side of the room. He walked to her, undoing his belt. Lilian wasted no time in driving the sharp glass into his exposed stomach. He cried out in surprise, falling to his knees. She yanked the glass back and drove it into his neck. As he lay dying, the basement door creaked open.

She never considered him to have a partner; she awaited a gunshot or to be charged at.

"Lilian?" It was her father.

"Dad!" she cried.

"You called me, but the connection was so bad." He embraced her; she felt the fabric of his shirt and smelled his cologne, knowing that he was real. "It sounded like you were under water. Then you sent me this house address." He looked her over, tears rolling down in stubble strewn face. "No wonder. What happened?"

"He took me, hit me over the head." Her father looked back at the body, and then to her.

"The police are on their way." As he embraced her again, a thought occurred to her; she hadn't had her phone with her. She had no way to call her father, nor did she remember doing so.

Jonah's Revenge

Chuck Baker

One of my fondest childhood memories is a day my Grandpa took me fishing. It was a warm spring day in April. April second, in fact. I remember the date, because Grandpa said we would have gone the day before, but it was April Fools' Day, and he didn't want me to think he was fooling about fishing.

He picked me up before lunch, and we drove three miles outside our small town to a farm pond owned by Grandpa's friend Wally. He parked close to the dam, and handed me an empty mayonnaise jar with holes punched in the lid. He asked me to catch grasshoppers to put in the jar while he unloaded the gear and set up our picnic lunch.

The grasshoppers were plentiful, and almost every one of them spit black goo on my hands as I put them in the jar. After a dozen or so, I was thirsty and asked how many more I needed. He said that was enough to start with, because he had brought some catfish bait.

While I was chasing insects, Grandpa baited two rods with chicken livers, cast them, and was sitting on the dam with a canteen of water.

As I set the jar down and settled in the soft greening grass, Grandpa baited the hook on a cane pole with a grasshopper, flipped it a few feet from the bank, and handed me the pole.

As soon as the bobber settled, it immediately disappeared, and Grandpa said, "Set the hook." I whipped the tip of the pole back and felt the quivering tug of a feisty sun perch bend the tip of the limber cane pole as I pulled the flopping fish onto the bank.

Grandpa took it off the hook, put it into a five gallon bucket half full of water, baited my hook, and tossed it back into the pond.

This routine repeated itself until we had six perch in the bucket. Then Grandpa said, " Let's bait the throw line." He picked up a long cord with six treble hooks attached about two feet apart and a huge bolt with a nut attached for a weight. One at a time, he snagged a perch on each hook, and when all hooks had bait, he looped the cord into his left hand, swung the weight over his head, and flung it as far into the pond as he could. He tied the cord to a railroad spike he had driven into the ground with a ball peen hammer and asked me if I was ready for lunch.

The salty slab of smoked ham wrapped in a piece of rye bread was very tasty and filled me past the point of having a piece of Grandma's mince meat pie, so Grandpa ate his and mine, then leaned forward to tighten the line on both rods.

The huge, fluffy, snow white clouds drifting overhead slowly changed shapes, with some forming familiar looking figures and others bulging into unidentifiable masses, when one of Grandpa's rod tips bent down hard in the forked stick it was resting in. He picked the rod up, jerked hard, and whatever was on the hook didn't seem to budge. He let the rod tip down, reeled several times, and jerked the rod back again.

Slowly, the catch was pulled toward the bank as he dropped the rod tip, reeled, and pulled the rod back over and over until the biggest catfish I had ever seen in all of my seven years was pulled up to the edge of the water. Holding the rod in one hand, he stood, grabbed the fish behind the gill, and lifted it on the bank.

I had never seen him so happy. He laughed, giggled, whooped, hollered, and said several times, "What a beauty."

After putting the huge fish on a stringer, baiting the hook, and casting as far as he could, Grandpa sat down, let out a sigh of satisfaction, and grinned like the canary that ate a cat.

Grandpa had never been so excited about anything. He was usually quiet and when he did say something, it always made people laugh. Grandpa was in such a good mood, I asked, "Grandpa, why do you like fishing so much?"

His big broad grin narrowed slightly, a look into the distance crossed his eyes and in a steady baritone voice, he stated, as if reading Shakespeare to a live audience, "Sonny, the reason I like fishing is because of the story of Jonah in the *Bible*. The most magnificent fish story I've ever heard."

I remembered the story of Jonah from *Bible* school last summer but couldn't equate that to the joy of fishing, so I asked, "Grandpa, why does Jonah being swallowed by a whale make you like to go fishing?"

A small glint came into his eyes as he focused on

my question and replied, "Sonny, when we go fishing, we throw bait in the water and hope a fish swallows it. In the story of Jonah, the sailors threw him in the water, and he got swallowed by a fish. The irony of that makes the story of Jonah the most fantastic fish story I've ever heard."

I didn't understand so I asked, "Grandpa, what is irony?"

He grinned and answered, "To me, irony is when something turns out the exact opposite of what is expected."

I understood that but was still curious, so I quizzed, "So irony makes you like to go fishing?"

That brought a chuckle as he chimed, "No, irony makes me laugh. The important thing I noticed while studying Jonah, was that God prepared the fish to swallow Jonah before he commanded him to go to Nineveh. God knows man does not have the ability to be obedient unless he has some help, so sometimes he makes things so difficult when we're disobedient, we sort of stumble onto the right path trying to escape the consequences, and I'm disobedient so often, I'm always trying to catch that big fish before it catches me."

Waylaid by Deodorant

Bernadette Lowe

Every day starts the same when you're in high school. Get dressed for school, eat breakfast, pick up your books, and head for the school bus. Every day holds some complication for an anxious teen. And so it was, in my junior year in high school, that anxiousness was a part of my every day. Back then, it was old fashioned "sweating" with deodorant that let our beads of anxiousness float through. We were not "Sure", we didn't know a thing about "Always", and our teen days weren't "Old Spice." But this one time, I felt a difference from the norm; something new did not feel good. It felt sticky and gooey. Moving one elbow away from my body, ever so slightly, I hoped no one noticed. It stuck, and it seemed to string away. It was horrible. I knew something was wrong.

Several school days went by, and I learned to gently flap my arms like a chicken. Here I was in high school, in panty hose and heels, trying to look like a cutey pie, and flapping my wings like a chicken to the side, since with every chance I got for air seemed to help. Desperate, I told Mom that something was wrong and asked if the deodorant was old. She confided to me that she had the same problem.

Nope, don't even think about it. My Mom did not flap her wings. She said she just felt glued. There was no money for new deodorant, especially since the can was not empty. Even if there had been money, we didn't go to town for a whim. It was only on Saturdays when Dad went to the feed store. A new can was not gonna fly with these good, but poor folks.

And so it was, that I continued using this stuff, knowing it was another flappy day in store. But one fine morning, as I squirted, it hit me hard between the eyes.

"Mom, Mom", I shrieked. She came running into the bathroom in short order, squirted, and confirmed my sniff test. Sure enough, somehow we had bought the only can of deodorant with hair spray. But no, Mom was smarter than the can and figured it out. This hadn't occurred when the can was new, only recently.

The lineup began. And the inquisition. For Mom was gonna get to the bottom of the can. Sure enough, Mom's sharp tongue and squinted eye noticed that one brother looked guilty. Clueing in on him, she aimed all that bent up frustration from being sticky right at his conscience till he 'fessed up. He'd been figured out, and we knew he did it. He had not told a soul what he had done.

He had taken off the little white round tip that had a hole for squirters on both the hair spray can and the deodorant cans. Matching the straw-like short sticks by holding the full hair spray can upside down on top of the empty deodorant can, he'd refilled the deodorant can with hair spray and then sat back and watched the action.

Oh, boy, he never did that again. Mom made sure in her own way. You see, Mom had an interest in this situation. It was personal for her. Can you imagine her arms glued together in church and squirming and not being able to figure it out? You know, she didn't like what Jimmy did. Anyway, good folks, refilling the cans works. I know. Trust me. It works real good. Don't try it, and if you do, make sure that you don't try it on your can of deodorant.

A Fish Story

Glenda Brown

If anyone ever had a fish story to tell, it is I, Lucy Jennings. It's not about the fish I caught; it's about a fish that caught a classmate many years ago. Recalling this story brings both joy and pain to days gone by where I sat behind this huge classmate who seemed much older than his years. This classmate was a boy named Lucas Pittman. He was eleven years old, the same as myself, and we were in Mrs. Stewart's sixth grade class at Washington Elementary School. There were twelve boys and six girls that year.

Most of my classmates were normal sixth graders who fit the role of a typical sixth grader from a small rural town. There were a few boys that were exceptional or should I say downright weird. Terry Sanderson, who I thought was the best looking boy in class, was my boyfriend. Only my best friend Dorothy Gail and I knew this. Terry was completely in the dark about my deep love for him and could not have cared less. He was not the least bit interested in girls. In fact, he wasn't interested in anything except a popular TV show about a dog called *Rin TinTin.*

Terry didn't do well in school. He could barely read. When Mrs. Stewart called on him to read orally, she would have to help him through it. Terry was very shy, and it bothered him terribly to read to the class. It hurt to see how he struggled.

His classmates couldn't feel too sorry for him, because he was drop dead gorgeous. Every girl in the sixth grade claimed that he was their boyfriend. Even Dorothy Gail behind my back.

Then there was James McHenry, who was the "potty mouth" of the class. He got into so much trouble from our teacher, because he used the phrase "the butt crack of dawn" with every sentence that came of out his mouth. He implemented it in all his language; even if it fit or not. He had such a potty mouth that Mrs. Stewart spent half her time trying to clean up his speech.

Then there was Kenneth Lawson, the prankster. He was not above sneaking under Mrs. Stewart desk and tying her shoe laces together. When she stood up and tried to walk, she fell. The class would roar with laughter until she got back on her feet and grabbed her thick wooden paddle. If she could figure out who did it, they were in deep trouble.

Mrs. Stewart was a wonderful teacher, but she had lots of problems with discipline. She was well on her way to a nervous breakdown trying to handle James McHenry alone.

Then there was Lucas. The oversized genius. Lucas was a big standout by his size and IQ. If you passed our classroom and looked in, you would have thought he didn't belong there. He just didn't fit in with the normal sized sixth graders. He was by far the smartest kid in our entire school.

I overheard the teachers discussing Lucas. They thought he was too bright for the sixth grade and that he should be promoted up a grade or two. His parents wouldn't allow this. They wanted Lucas to stay in his age group, even though they knew he was bored.

Saying Lucas was smart was an understatement. Lucas had this giant vocabulary, and we all learned from just listening to him speak. Lucas also possessed a big booming voice and was easily heard all over the room. Sometimes Mrs. Stewart would let him read a novel to the class. He could pronounce any word and seemed to know its meaning.

He used the word *platonic* one morning while referring to a story he had just read. Mrs. Stewart asked the class to raise their hands if they knew the meaning of the word. James McHenry was the first to raise his bony hand. Mrs. Stewart made him put it down before he could say anything stupid. None of us knew what it meant, and we were positive that James McHenry would not be giving us the true definition.

After Mrs. Stewart silenced James, Lucas explained to us that it meant a relationship between a boy and a girl that was only friendship. No romance. James McHenry told the class he knew exactly the meaning of the word, but his freedom of speech had been taken away. Mrs. Stewart took both James McHenry and his desk to the hallway where he stayed the rest of the day making paper airplanes and throwing them back into our classroom.

Whether Lucas was a genius or not, I don't know. At eleven years old, he wore a size 11 men's shoe. He was taller than our teacher Mrs. Stewart, who stood 5'9 inches tall. Lucas was terribly overweight. Obese, you could call it. He bought his clothes in the men's department and wore them loose to make himself seem smaller. His eating habits, no doubt, played a big part.

Every morning, Lucas went across the street to Trueduea's Grocery store and bought $1.00 worth of candy. Back in the 50s, a $1.00 worth of candy was a lot of candy. He had it eaten by lunch time. Then he got out the enormous lunch that his over protective mother packed, making sure her only child did not go hungry at school. After all the candy, two peanut butter and jelly sandwiches plus a thermos of chocolate milk, he would often get a belly ache. This belly ache became so common that Ms. Stewart placed a trash can beside Lucas's desk, so that he could barf in it and not in the floor. His barfing episodes would come and go so quickly, it was the only thing Mrs. Stewart could do to handle it.

Because of this barfing we nicknamed him "Lucas Pukus", of course, behind his back. No one had the nerve to say it to his face. Lucas was not someone to mess with. He definitely was not a bully, but he was quick to defend himself, especially if he thought someone was making a joke of his size.

I became a true friend to Lucas one morning during our pledge of allegiance to the flag. When Lucas stood up to salute the flag, a condom fell down the leg of his loosely fitting pants and landed on the floor. I noticed he had been walking sort of strange that morning. Now I knew why. I was totally floored that he would do such a stupid thing.

What could he possibly be thinking?

I couldn't stand the thought of the humiliation that would follow if anyone saw it. I saw a chance to retrieve the soft icky thing along with a pencil that had fallen under his desk. Quickly moving, I grabbed up the pencil and used it to retrieve the condom. \When Lucas saw it hanging from the end of the pencil, his face turned white. I quickly open my lunch box which was tucked in my desk along with my text books. I slipped the condom underneath my sandwich.

No one noticed my fidgeting. Everyone was watching James McHenry. When lunch time came, I just sat there and read my library book. Dorothy Gail asked me why I wasn't eating my lunch. I told her I wasn't hungry. That was a big lie. I was starving. She then asked if she could have my dessert. I told her no. She gave me a dirty look then returned to her seat, but that was a much better situation then giving her a peek inside my lunchbox. I would settle with her later on, but for right now I had to make it through lunch time.

Now, I'm not a dumb girl for eleven years old. I know all about the birds and bees, but at the same time, I did not want to take any kind of chances eating a contaminated sandwich and getting pregnant. My mother told me a girl can't be too careful around boys... I knew she had prepared me for times like this. The day seemed to go on forever and ever. I couldn't take my mind off the lunch box and its seedy contents.

When it was finally time to go home Lucas turned to me and said "be careful." He knew that thing was still in my lunchbox.

On my way to the bus, I ran passed a trash bin that smelled awful. I knew this would be the place to dispose of the contents of my lunchbox. Looking around to make sure no one was watching, I stood on my tiptoes to reach the top of the trash bin. Then, I quickly dumped all evidence. I felt so relieved with my empty lunchbox. I felt a big burden had been lifted. Now I could breathe. I can remember only one other incident involving Lucas that was so terrifying it probably took a few years off my life. I probably would not have done this for anyone else, but I was determined to show Lucas I was a true friend no matter the circumstances. In a way, I felt Lucas was family. I can't explain exactly why.

I went to Lucas's house pretty often, because my mother worked as a housekeeper for his mother Mrs. Pittman. She was a very generous woman who overpaid my mother because she knew we needed the money. On this particular Friday afternoon, I rode the bus home with Lucas. My mother was cleaning Mrs. Pittman's house that day.

I wanted to go home with my best friend, Dorothy Gail, because she had discovered a new hair product called "Get Set," and I wanted her to fix my hair just like hers. All the pleading didn't work, so I had to ride the bus home with Lucas. It was necessary to keep him company while Mom cleaned the house. She needed me to keep him occupied, so he would not following her around talking non-stop about everything or wanting her to stop and make him some chocolate pudding, which was his favorite food in all the world.

I wasn't too embarrassed riding the bus home with Lucas. The kids knew that my mother worked as his housekeeper, so I was pretty sure they thought nothing of it. As I took a seat next to Lucas, I hoped my disappointment wasn't showing. Deep down, I felt I owed Lucas my friendship, because his mother was so good to our family.

Immediately after we got to his house that Friday afternoon, Lucas had the bright idea he wanted to go fishing. It was still early afternoon, because on Friday we got out of school at 2:15 It was around 3 o'clock when we gathered our fishing gear and started for the creek that was about a mile behind his house. We had fished there many times before, sometimes with his dad.

It was mid April, and it had rained some that morning giving the air a cold chill. Lucas said it would be a great day for fishing, because it had sprinkled lightly. According to him this would make the fish come to the surface and be easy fishing. I pretty much believed everything Lucas said.

On the way to the creek, we ran into old Mr. Miller who was out in his cow pasture looking for space ships. Lucas told me to say hi and be polite but not to start a conversation with him, because he was ninety-five years old and BATSH** crazy. I took his advice, and we moved quickly passed him with just a sweet hello.

We were getting situated on the creek bank when Lucas Pukus came up with another brilliant idea.

"Let's go skinny dipping!" he said.

I was shocked out of my mind when I heard him suggest such a thing. I had just started wearing a bra, and I wasn't about to get naked with any boy, let alone Lucas Pukus.

"Definitely not!" I yelled at him. Regardless of my begging him not to, he peeled off his loose fitting pants.

I closed my eyes and put my hands over most of my face. I must admit I peeked a little, just to make sure he was actually taking off his clothes. I caught a quick glimpse of his backside. Then I heard an enormous splash. His huge body hit the water like a cannon. Wave after wave came rolling toward the bank. He came up shrieking and yelling about how exhilarating the freezing water felt.

"Come on," he coaxed. He would not let up on me… I was really beginning to panic…

"I don't want you to see me naked!" I yelled back at him. I couldn't believe our fishing trip had taken this turn. What did Lucas think he was doing?

I tried to ignore him, but he kept yelling loudly, " I know you looked at me! Come on, say you looked!" Lucas had this way of making someone answer his questions, because he never let up until he had his way. "You saw me, didn't you?" He sounded like his mouth was half full of water. This is not Lucas Pukus, I thought. This is some crazy boy. I was still reeling from shock, knowing he was in the creek without any clothes on. Apparently, he had lost his mind.

He kept giggling as he bobbed up and down in the cold water. I tried to answer appropriately, so I said to him, "Yes, I saw you, but all I saw was the butt crack of dawn!" I couldn't have said it better. He knew exactly what I meant. The laughter continued on, with him trying to persuade me to jump into the water.

I finally caved and plunged in with all my clothes on. I immediately regretted my insane decision. The icy cold water gripped my whole being into agony beyond belief. I was coming up for air when I heard him scream. This was not an ordinary scream, it was an "I'm in trouble!" kind of scream. A scream of pure terror.

Wiping the icy water out of my face, I could see Lucas struggled to get out of the water. He had made it to mid- thigh depth, and I could see him flailing at something between his legs. Then I saw a large fish swim away at the surface. Lucas continued to scream bloody murder as he made his way to creek bank. Terrified, I followed.

He pulled himself out of the water still holding his crotch. He did not stop to pick up his clothes. He was running as fast as he could back toward his house. I grabbed up his clothes and began running after him.

I knew something terrible had happened with the fish, so I yelled, "Is it all there?"

He yelled back, "Shut up!"

About half way between the house and the creek, we ran past old Mr. Miller who was just standing there with both hands on his hips and his mouth wide open. He never uttered a word or at least I didn't hear him. I am sure it was not every day that he saw a naked boy running through his cow pasture with a girl chasing after him. I wasn't the least bit worried about what old Mr. Miller saw. He was over ninety and convinced his cows were spaceships.

I finally made it to the gate when I saw Lucas run through his back door. As I paused to catch my breath, I could hear Lucas screaming and howling to my mother about what happened. At this point, I was so scared I could feel my heart beating out of my chest.

I fell to my knees at the gate and stayed there until I heard my mother say, "Come on, get in the car."

After an emergency trip to the doctor's office, we learned that Lucas was fine. He had some big bite marks but Lucas was still all in one piece, thank God.

Lots of things began to happen the last two months of school. Terry Sanderson was moving to Tennessee and would not be coming back. I didn't know if I could survive without him. Dorothy Gail was spending the summer with her grandmother in Dallas, Texas.

Mrs. Stewart tearfully told us that the she would not be teaching at Washington Elementary the coming fall. The school did not renew her contract. Everyone knew she had a big discipline problem. She cried a lot, and we all tried to cheer her up the best we could, telling her what a great teacher she was and that we would never forget her. I felt really sad until the final day of school.

Lucas's demeanor had been very quiet. Everyone had noticed the change. When asked if I knew what was bothering him, I said I had no idea. His secrets were safe with me. I knew he was scared that I had told the other classmates about the fish. I had not breathed a word to anyone.

It was while we were putting up the books for the

end of the year that he walked up to me and slipped a note in my hand. I opened the note and read it quickly.

It said, "I've never had a better friend then you—platonic, that is." I quickly tucked the note inside my trusty lunchbox which could hold any secret. He started to say something but changed his mind. He stood there for a few minutes, just looking at me with this big smile. I shall never forget this smile.

Little Monster

Kandy Anderson

I want to be scary
Really, I do.

I'm going to grow big
And come after you

When I get my teeth
You just watch out

I'm going to make you
Scream and shout

I'm the monster you wish you were
I understand if you're a little disturbed

You just wait I got a plan
I'm going to make you poop your pants

Watch me growl with my new teeth
And see who has a problem with sleep

So hold that cutie and cuchi cuchi coo
Cuz I'm that bump in the night that goes BOO!

My Summer Gift

Connie Sweeney

Time spent in the summers on my grandparents' farm was something special. Really, really special. Having grown up in a residential area in a small town, I relished the experiences of farm life when I stayed with my grandparents on summer breaks.

From age six through eleven, I looked forward to it beginning in spring every year, hoping with all my being that I would be allowed to go for a few days that summer. It usually wasn't hard to convince my parents that I HAD to go; there were only a couple of my childhood summers I had to skip for some family reason or other.

This summer was going to be the best so far! I just knew it. I was nine years old and felt that I was worldly enough to pack all kinds of exciting activities into the six days I had been allotted on the farm. My parents drove me halfway, meeting my grandparents and moving my bags from one vehicle to the other.

Quickly dismissing my mom and dad with a kiss, I jumped in the backseat of my grandparent's pickup, and away we went. They were old-fashioned farmers, routinely trading pickups every year before the vehicle wore out from the daily wear and tear of farm life, so it was always fun to see what pickup they showed up in.

Somewhere along the way, I drifted off into a

nap, exhausted from the anticipation of the trip. I awoke to my grandfather saying, "Well, she has gained a little weight since last summer. I hope she doesn't get fat."

What? Ouch, that hurts, I thought to myself. Okay, so maybe I had been eating more fried bologna sandwiches right after school than usual, but fat? Really? I kept quiet, embarrassed to have overheard that remark.

In her defense, my grandma admonished Grandpa, saying, "Now, Ralph," and she let it go at that.

That should have been my first red flag that this summer was going to have a strange twist, but I chose to ignore the thought.

It was dark by the time we arrived and suppertime. After eating, I wandered through the house, nosing into nooks and crannies to see what had changed since last summer. Falling into bed at my grandma's house felt so nice. I swear she ironed the bed sheets.

I awoke to a rooster crowing and quickly got dressed for my farm adventures. After eating a huge homemade breakfast of ham, eggs, and toast, I was set for the day. Manners had been drilled into me, so I helped Grandma clean the kitchen. It seemed to me that the woman was always in the kitchen. If she wasn't outside helping Grandpa do some outside chore, her time was spent cooking everything from scratch for the two of them. This week, it would be for the three of us, so I felt obligated to pitch in and help her. Looking back, I don't know how much help I was, since I was too short to reach much in her kitchen, but at least I put forth the effort.

Grandpa had already left in the old farm truck they

kept specifically for checking cattle, so I missed out on that trip. But I wasn't deterred; I knew I'd have a blast in the barnyard.

The old-fashioned things that they used fascinated me. I loved the washhouse with Grandma's wringer washing machine. I wasn't entirely sure how the whole contraption worked, but I knew the clothes were fed in between two rollers, and you had to turn the crank handle for a bit, and the clothes came out the other side flat, somewhat drier and clean. I gave that thing a wide berth, remembering how my sister had somehow gotten her hand stuck in the thing just the summer before. The drain in the middle of the floor was also scary to me, although now I can't say why. It always smelled damp and clean in that building.

Grandma's clothesline was different than the one we had, and she used hers every day. We had a clothesline, only for the sheets or really big items. I spent a lot of time weaving in and out of Grandpa and Grandma's clothing, relishing the scents and pretending I was hidden from anyone's sight.

When Grandma came out of the house, I knew I could venture from the fenced yard, and the real exploring soon came. She had her daily chores, so we went first to the henhouse. Just to be able to walk across the barnyard was a thrill to me. I loved exploring around the old wooden buildings and silos. I had been taught not to go too far, so she allowed me to wander on my own.

Something in the corral caught my eye, and in an instant, joy filled my heart. A new foal stood by her mother, watching us make our way to them. "Here's your surprise," my grandma said.

"Oh my gosh, you didn't tell me you had a new baby filly!" I squealed with pleasure. My grandparents knew how horse crazy I was. Every year I spent the majority of my visit fussing over their two horses. Butch and Lady appreciated every carrot I fed them and every brushing I gave them. Grandma and Grandpa spoiled those two, but anytime I was there they got extra doses of love.

"Lady had this little one three weeks ago, and I wanted to wait until you got here to surprise you," my grandma explained. "Her name is Star."

I now knew why I was there - it was to take care of the new foal. Even though I was a mere nine years old, I was certain my future involved horses, either making a living with them or at least owning several when I got my own place. My love for horses began at the farm with Butch and Lady, then grew each time I read every book about horses I could check out at the library. My favorite at that time was the *Black Beauty* series; I actually owned a couple of those books, and I treasured them.

As I relied on my very well-honed nine year-old instincts for horses, (of course, I knew everything about them didn't I) I felt that Star and I immediately bonded. She looked at me, I looked at her, and the world shifted. She gave her heart and soul to me, I just knew it. And she had my heart at first glance. Well, that may not have been reality, but it was what I chose to believe in that moment.

Forgetting about going to the henhouse with Grandma, I scrambled over the wood corral railings to get closer to my new best friend. Grandma said, "Now wait, slow down, she doesn't know you. And Lady is very protective. It's her baby."

"Okay, it'll be fine," I mumbled as I climbed into the corral.

Lady raised her head to see who dared to approach her Star. "It's okay, Lady, it's me," I said soothingly. She shook her head slightly and gave me the green light to approach. Star anxiously stepped behind her mother, unsure of me. I spent most of my time that first day petting Lady, rubbing her mane and talking to her. Our main subject was, of course, Star. The filly glanced at me from under Lady's neck and around her swishing tail. I guessed she was as curious about me as I was about her. I had never actually been that close to a new foal, and I couldn't wait to get my hands on her.

After almost thirty minutes passed, my grandma surely got tired of waiting around for me. She had collected the eggs from the hens in the henhouse and stood watching me. The fact that I skipped that chore did not escape either of us, as that was my other favorite thing to do, although not by myself. I made sure someone went in before me, after my dad saw a snake in one of the coops. Apparently, the snakes had a fondness for eggs and routinely robbed the chickens of their offerings before my grandparents could collect them. Still, it was a thrill to see how many eggs the hens left for us each day.

"Okay, let's leave the horses for awhile and let them rest," Grandma decided.

"Oh, just a second longer," I begged.

Indulging me, Grandma allowed me to stay inside the corral for another few minutes as she walked toward the house. Finally, she said, "Come on, let's go make some cookies."

Reluctantly, I made my way over the wide wooden railing, out of the corral, and back to the house. I was pretty thirsty and could certainly eat some of Grandma's fresh homemade cookies, but that still that paled when compared to actually petting and spending time with my new Star.

By the time I got free of my grandparents watchful eyes, it was dusk. Star was lying on straw hay in the corner of the corral, with Lady watching over her. I couldn't decide whether to enter the corral and play with her or let her rest, so I just stood and stared. I stood silently until she fell asleep, at which point I fell even more in love with her. She was so pretty, her fur so soft and her face so sweet.

Dark in the country can get pretty scary for a city kid. I finally left the sleeping baby and her mother, and went inside. Exhausted from my first day at the farm, I went to bed early and dreamed of my future with Star. I dreamed that we spent the rest of our lives together, horse and owner, best friends. I dreamed of me riding her across fields and streams, of us quietly visiting at the end of a day. Our lives would be perfect.

Daybreak does come early at my grandparent's house, with the rooster crowing and luscious breakfast smells wafting from the kitchen. I really was happy to see my grandparents and spend time with them. We had a very enjoyable breakfast together. They both quizzed me about school, my mom, dad, and sister and Tippy my dog. But, honestly, we all three knew I couldn't wait to run outside to visit with Star.

After cleaning the kitchen and making my bed, I hot-footed it to the corral to see Star. Normally feeding Butch his oats for the day with Grandpa was one of my favorite chores. Today, not so much. I told Butch hi, petted him for a second while dumping his oats in the horse trough. I heard my grandma say, "I'll be in the wash-house for a bit, and Grandpa is going to County Line to get a part for the tractor."

Certain that my day spent with Star was going to be blissful, I hardly heard her words.

I spotted both Lady and Star and jumped up onto the railing. *She's such a cutie*, I thought. Both horses raised their heads and watched me watching them. I stood it as long as I could, then decided it would be just fine for me to get in the corral with Star. The rule at the farm was that I didn't get into the corral with Butch or Lady without an adult, but, I reasoned, it was just Star, and she and I were already besties!

Climbing down onto the dirt, I called to Star. She seemed really interested in me. *In fact*, I thought, *here she comes, right to me!*

Lady saw that it was only me and went back to eating her serving of breakfast oats. But Star was enchanted with me, focusing on me from across the corral. I started walking to her, and she started towards me.

I'm not sure what caused the ruckus, but all of the sudden Star jumped sideways and began running. Running right towards me – as if she couldn't wait any longer. For some reason, she looked bigger to me as she kicked her heels up, bucked and snorted. The closer she came to me, the bigger she looked. Time seemed to stop as the filly became more excited. I stopped moving as she broke into a full-out run. It was as though she had lost control of her long legs, and those hooves began to look dangerous as they were being waved about in the air. Those legs and hooves were coming closer and closer, and the closer they got, the more I began to (dare I say it?), change my mind about being besties with Star. I wondered if she had become possessed, because that's how she looked as she tossed her head and her behind at the same time. Even her eyes got bigger!

I stood still as long as I could, but fear made my legs move me out of the path of the oncoming onslaught of that wild animal. I began running, unsure where exactly to head to, but somewhere, anywhere! I looked over my shoulder, and unbelievably, it appeared that my running had only energized Star! The more I ran, the more she ran towards me. By this point, I was terrified, fortunately not frozen with fear, but horrified that I was about to die by foal thrashing.

Gasping for breath, I reached the railing and hauled myself up to the top. *Safe! I've saved myself. Hmm -that's weird, I don't hear her coming,* I thought to myself, turning around once I was out of her reach.

I looked, and Star was standing directly in front of me, stock-still and staring.

My grandma strolled up. "I saw you two playing

together. Are you having fun?" she questioned.

"Playing?" I said incredulously. "She wanted to kill me!" I yelled.

"Oh goodness no," Grandma stated calmly. "She just wants you to play with her, and she doesn't realize she's any bigger than you," she explained.

Well, now that made sense to me. She was young, and so was I. And of course, she wanted to run and play. So I forgave her for the terrifying few minutes of our first encounter, and we played together every minute of the next five days. I also got several extra visits that year, because after all, she was mine and I was hers.

The Dreaded Gym Class

Charlotte Morse Cooper

When I was young, I was not popular or in one of the "in" crowds. I must say, though, that the few friends I had were very good friends, and we remain friends even to this day.

In the late 1960s and early 1970s, my family lived in Westminster, California. My siblings and I attended 17th Street Elementary School. When grade school ended for me, most of the kids I had gone to school with went to Warner Junior High. I literally lived on the wrong side of the railroad tracks on Trask Avenue and wound up attending Johnson Junior High. After awhile I made a few new friends.

The most distasteful change going from grade school to junior high and then to high school was gym class. We had to undress and shower with all the other girls. It seemed to me we spent more time undressing and showering than doing anything else. Some of the girls were more developed and sure of themselves than others. I was the one who ran through the shower and got just wet enough to need a towel, and I was one of the first girls to re-dress. I still remember the smell of forty deodorants that would permeate the dressing room air and burn the inside of our nostrils.

By eighth grade I just didn't care anymore. I

remember two girls who seemed to have perpetual menstrual periods. (If we were having a period, we were dismissed from participating in gym.) One of the PE teachers would go so far as to pull out our panties to see if we were wearing a belt and pad. After the teacher sent letters home to their mothers suggesting a trip to the gynecologist, these girls, too, became part of the naked masses.

After eighth grade three junior high schools dumped into Westminster High School, a large sprawling place. One end of the campus consisted of two stories. My locker was on the second floor. The gym was at the opposite side of the school, so I was always in a hurry to get there. Gym was also my last class of the day, and I dreaded it as much as anyone possibly could.

I knocked over every hurdle on the race track and was the last pick for softball. Whenever I ran I got a 'catch' in my side that made me think I'd have to die to get better. Even the shin guards we wore for field hockey failed to protect me; I would get bruises above the shields.

Basketball frightened me. The big girls would chase me; and I thought, if they want the ball so bad, they can have the damn thing, and I would give it to them. To say I was not athletic would be an understatement.

The worst of the worst, though, was swimming. The school swimming pool was outdoors. It wasn't that I couldn't swim; I actually enjoyed swimming. But there were diving boards—dun...dun...DUN...dun—three levels of them! I have a fear of heights that would paralyze me, statue-stiff looking down from the board to the water below. To make matters worse, being the last class of the day, swimsuits would be depleted and the sizes were whatever was available.

The seniors were first in line, and we lowly freshmen were the tail end. We would go to the cage where a girl would ask our size. Why they bothered to ask I truly do not know; they never had the correct size.

The girl in the cage would say "Size?"

I would say "10."

The girl in the cage would say "Take a 16."

I am also not sure what fabric those red swimsuits were made of, but it stretched when it got wet and the lower portion of my swimsuit would feel as if I were swimming with a 1-pound bag of sand trailing behind each cheek. We girls would take the shoelaces out of our gym shoes and tie up the backs of our swimsuits to prevent our tops from slipping down and making us look like something from a porn movie. The weight of the swimsuits, when wet, also made it difficult for us to exit the pool while also trying to hold the swimsuits up at the same time.

The teacher announced one day that we could not pass the class without jumping from at least the medium board. The other girls got it over with quickly. But me…? I would go to the edge of the board every day and look down at the water, thinking it surely went into some sort of abyss from which I couldn't possibly swim back up to the top. The very last day of class, I once again climbed to the edge of the board, holding my suit up and looking downward. It was foggy outside that day and therefore harder to see the bottom of the pool.

One, two, three…deep breath; one, two three…I jumped! I hit the water and bobbed to the surface to the thunderous applause of the teacher, who cried, "You did it, Morse! You did it!"

I went home and told my mother and grandmother of my success! The feeling was grand!

I have never jumped off a diving board since, nor do I ever intend to.

In my sophomore year, my family moved to El Reno, Oklahoma, and my anxiety over gym class abated. We stayed inside in the gym room and didn't have to undress anymore or take showers at my school. There was less competition in sports, and no more nudity. My gym teacher, Mrs. Marilyn Bruce, was very nice. To this day, I have a friendship with her on Facebook.

Grandma, the Rooster and the Outhouse

Karen Bullock

The adults languished in the house while the sounds of children playing drifted in the windows with the slight breeze. I, too, had been banished to the yard but had sneaked back to listen to my relatives as they talked and nibbled on the leftovers from the country lunch. I loved listening to the adults talk. They were so much more interesting than kids my age, and besides, you always got the juiciest tidbits of information while eavesdropping.

There was another reason I wanted to be in the airless, hot, little house. It was more ominous than covertly listening to the prattle of Grandma, my parents and other relatives.

My grandma's yard harbored a monster, a bogeyman dressed in white feathers. It was her prize Leghorn rooster. His flock pecked their way back and forth across Grandma's yard under his watchful, beady eye. He guarded them with relentless energy. Any disruption of the peaceful grazing of his hens would meet swift and painful justice. He would peck, flog and verbally attack whatever or whomever into submission. Then his boastful, loud, triumphant cries would alert the neighborhood declaring another misdeed had been properly punished. He was judge, jury and executioner jammed in a strutting, two foot mass of muscle, plumage, claws and beak.

For Grandma, he was her pride and joy, a champion and protector of her priceless hens. For me, he was the troll that lived under the bridge, the wicked witch of the West and the bogeyman that hid under all children's bed or lived in their closets. I feared him with the passion known only to little kids.

As in fairy tales, this monster had taken an instant dislike to me. Within minutes of arriving at Grandma's, I needed to use the bathroom. Grandma's house was not quite modern. In fact, that's why we were there, so "Her Boys" could build her a new-fangled bathroom, complete with running water and a toilet that flushed. Meanwhile, if you needed to use the "facilities," you had to go to the outhouse, and the outhouse was prime pecking territory of the hens.

On my way to the outhouse, I scared a hen. She cackled as she bolted from me. That was all it took. The rooster raced toward me, squawked my sentence and proceeded to beat me with his massive wings and peck at my head with his pointy, deadly beak. I was in the grip of a devil. Tufts of hair flew, and I screamed. From that time on, when I needed to go to the outhouse, I had to do battle with the rooster. My family was no help. They teased me about the horrific attack, making the rooster larger than real-life. My monster grew with each gibe, and fear made the trips to the outhouse more common than normal.

So I did the only thing a small kid can do. I asked my shining knight to fight the dragon for me. My dad accepted the dubious honor of escorting me to-and-from the outhouse. With the grace of any knight, he shooed the hens from our path and held off the rooster while I finished my task; then he would swing me up on his shoulders and carry me back to the house, challenging the rooster the whole way. Unfortunately, fighting monsters was not his only job. The progress of the new bathroom slowed as Dad fought my dragon. I would announce my need and hop from one foot to the other, uttering whines of "Now, Daddy, now" until Dad would relent.

It was during one of these dances Dad made THE PRONOUNCEMENT he would regret. "Damn it, Karen, get a stick, and when he comes at you, hit him as hard as you can! I don't have the time to keep hauling you back and forth to the bathroom!" He meant it. My white knight had surrendered. I was on my own, and the monster still lurked in the yard.

I thought I could out-wait either Dad or the rooster. I hopped around, watched TV and even helped in the kitchen, anything to keep my mind from thinking of the pressure in my bladder. But my need was too great. The moment of truth had come. I stoically stepped out onto the porch. Sure enough, the rooster was between me and the outhouse. There was no escape. I spied a small two by four — a scrap from the new bathroom — picked it up and moved out on the lawn, clutching the board like a bat. The rooster saw me, squawked his hellish cry and made his charge. When he was in range, I swung.

My world erupted in a mass of blood and white feathers. I screamed. The now-headless chicken was still exacting his revenge on me. I stood rooted to my spot on the lawn screaming, blood pouring down my face and urine flowing down my legs. Dad was the first to reach me.

Believing the rooster had pecked my eyes out (which I am sure it would have done if it still had a head) he rushed me into the house, held me in the sink and turned the water on full-force. The screams ceased as the gurgles began. It was not enough I had been attacked by the rooster; now my own father was trying to drown me!

Satisfied both eyes were still intact, he sat me down in a sodden mess on the kitchen floor. Water, tears, urine and feathers dripped onto the patterned linoleum.

It was at this time, Grandma began hollering for him. "Now what?" he demanded.

"Billy, come here and look what your daughter has done to my rooster," Grandma dictated. "She killed my prize rooster!"

Dad's laughter cut through her complaints, and he looked at me, quivering as I sat on the floor in an every-growing puddle.

"What did you hit him with?" He asked still chuckling.

"A board I found on the porch", I mewed, worried of the punishment to come.

"A board? Dammit, Karen, I told you a stick!"

"What's the difference?" I innocently asked.

"I guess the difference is a live rooster and a dead one."

I cleaned up. Grandma was mad at me, I could tell by the way she pursed her lips when I'd get around her.

I'd embarrassed myself by wetting my pants, and Dad had near drowned me.

Things couldn't get much worse, but it did. Supper was served. The guest-of-honor took his rightful place. The Leghorn rooster, cut up and swimming in chicken broth with homemade dumplings, sat in a large pot in the center of the table. I gagged on the first bite and asked to leave the table. There would be no supper for me.

The new bathroom was finished in a couple of days. I knew I was back in Grandma's good graces when she let me be the first one to use it. The toilet seat was smoother than the one in the outhouse, and it flushed. Grandma was in seventh heaven. But my greatest delight was the absence of the Leghorn rooster or any other monsters. Of course, I never opened the bathroom cupboard door. But that's another story.

A Lesson in Girl-Power

Clay Fees

In the summer of 1989, I was sixteen years old, and I was a high school junior in the small Oklahoma Route 66 town of Kellyville. It is not one of the towns you will read about in the unending stream of books on Route 66 and is known to posterity for nothing except a stillborn attempt to create Oklahoma's only ski resort outside of town. True story, but I digress...

Like most sixteen year old high school students, I was struggling to find an identity. I didn't fit well into any of the various cliques that inevitably develop in even the smallest of schools. I was an athlete, primarily of baseball, so that made me a bit of a square peg in the nerd group, despite my astounding skill at *Dungeons and Dragons*. That same *Dungeons and Dragons* skill coupled with the fact that I could read and enjoyed doing so made me a bit of a misfit in the jock club. My family raised horses and cattle, so the Vo-Ag group was an option, but I wasn't as dedicated as some to agribusiness as it was practiced in Kellyville. I was sort of a social jack-of-all-trades – I could move in various social circles, but the movements were awkward, similar to my ability to dance.

One thing I certainly did have going for me was my car. A couple of summers before, my dad bought me a bona fide muscle car, a 1968 Plymouth Road Runner.

Looking back, it was a mechanical turd, but for me in 1989, it was the one cool thing I could hang my hat on. When it deigned to run, that is. By 1989, it wore fresh a coat of red paint with black hood stripes, courtesy of my uncle, and it sported a 375 horsepower, 440 cubic inch engine and four-speed manual transmission. Driving that car I would have been Burt Reynolds – albeit with a much less impressive moustache – had it been 1970, but it still gave me a modicum of coolness in 1989.

That car sort of became my identity. My main attribute as a baseball player was my speed - I'd go on to lead the state in stolen bases the following two springs – so naturally my nickname became "Road Runner". To this day, when I go back to Kellyville, inevitably someone will refer to me by that name.

That old car was very fast. By all measures of technology and style, it was a holdover from another era, but in the late 1980s, an era starved of automotive performance, it was still very quick. I spent many afternoons beating the crap out of my colleagues at Kellyville High on a makeshift drag strip outside of town. With the exception of Eric Stubblefield in his beat up old 327 powered '72 Chevy pickup, most people only raced me once. Eric was a bit of a slow study. I'd drive that car into Sapulpa on Friday and Saturday nights to cruise the loop, seeking out victims for my Road Runner to devour. Before too long, my big Plymouth cruiser was the terror of Creek County among the dying breed of high school drag racers, ourselves scions of a dying era.

That fall, when school started again, I was hanging out in the parking lot before school with my buddies, Tommy Turner and Ross McGuire. It was an annual ritual – we'd hang out in the parking lot and scout any new students of the female persuasion, or see if any of the old ones had gone through enough of a miraculous transformation over the summer to earn a place on our radars. Tommy, who was a car guy and a street racer himself, piloting a warmed up '70 Pontiac LeMans, and I would also see if any of the new driver's license holders rolled into the parking lot in an interesting car, someone who needed to be taken out to Slick Road and taught that that red Plymouth was King Stud in that parking lot.

Standing in the parking lot that morning, we heard, before we saw, just such an interesting car. The car that rumbled into the parking lot that morning was a 1970 Chevrolet Camaro, with white "SS" badging adorning the middle of its gaping maw of a grille. It was white - a generous description of its color, since it was also heavily adorned with copious amounts of rust and not a few dents. Tommy and I watched as the Super Sport growled its way to a parking spot. It sounded good. The door opened, screaming in protest from worn out door hinges, and out stepped Sandy Holmes.

Sandy had gone to school with us since kindergarten, and everyone knew her. Sandy was a pretty but unassuming girl, quiet and with no identifiable cliques. She didn't date anyone from Kellyville, though that wasn't because of a lack of interest, and rumor had it that she had a boyfriend down 66 in Bristow. She played basketball, but she generally went unnoticed. I don't think I had a conversation with her. Sandy was a lot like the cinder-block walls of the school – we knew they existed, but didn't think much about them. She was just sort of "there".

Sandy might have been unremarkable, but that SS wasn't, and Tommy and I took note of that car. Early on in the school year, we started in on her about coming out to Slick Road to race. She always timidly declined. This made us even more obnoxious, as we ratcheted up our taunting. People had started talking, and the talk was that Sandy's car was pretty quick, and she did a lot of racing in Bristow. I believed neither. I believed neither, because, you see, Sandy was a girl.

The immutable laws of biology dictate that a girl could not drive a fast car, at least not with any control, and if one was some sort of mutant and did competently drive a fast car, it was because some male taught her how. Regardless, girls certainly couldn't race. Racing was a skill, the mastering of which was precluded by ovaries. It required precision and timing – not the kind of precision and timing that went into, say, baking a pie, but the mechanical kind that was entirely unobtainable by anyone requiring a bra.

As time went on, we learned more about Sandy's car. It was a genuine '70 SS Camaro, with its factory supplied 396 under the hood, mated to a four-speed transmission. Sandy's dad bought it new before being awarded an all-expense paid vacation to Southeast Asia, courtesy of Lyndon Johnson and the US Army. That vacation left him paralyzed from the waist down, thanks to Viet Cong guerillas that preferred he vacation elsewhere, and he never drove his Camaro again. Before Vietnam, he was what used to be known in the '60s as a "grease monkey", and he knew his cars. From his wheelchair, he instructed Sandy on how to rebuild the engine, transmission and rear end of that 396, and she meticulously put it together, every bolt. Rumor had it that the result was one very quick little car.

To me, none of this added up. If the car was indeed quick, it had to be her younger brother Shawn who did the driving. He was equipped with testicles and therefore qualified, whereas Sandy most certainly was not. I refused to believe a girl could build any engine, much less one that ran well, whoever her tutor might have been. If Sandy was beating people in Bristow, they were either cars driven by other girls on some gyno-racing circuit, or by boys who were letting Sandy win in the furtherance of ulterior goals.

I had no ulterior designs on Sandy – I barely knew her name - so if I could ever coerce her into racing me, it would be simply put her in her place, which by my reckoning, was somewhere near the kitchen. By the spring of 1990, the growing consensus was that perhaps my Plymouth wasn't the king of the county anymore, and the mighty red Road Runner could be beaten by, of all things, a GIRL in a Camaro. So I stepped up my campaign of ridicule, to such an extent that by that following March Sandy angrily took me up on my offer.

I finally got my showdown. Not only would I make scrap metal of Sandy and her little Camaro and quell those rumors, but even more importantly, I would carry the banner of masculinity and smite the uppity female who had the temerity to venture into the no-girls-allowed world of street racing. I didn't enroll in Home Ec, and Sandy shouldn't have been racing people. That was the way the world was supposed to work.

I should have known something was amiss when I saw Sandy in the parking lot, wrenching around on something under her hood, but I figured she might have dropped a feminine hygiene product in there. She had a tool box sitting on her fender, unconcerned about any potential damage to the finish. In truth, she shouldn't have been; her car was a disaster from the outside, seemingly held together with baling wire and hope. She also had her brother Shawn hard at work, portable floor jack under the differential, swapping out rear tires. Sandy carried a portable jack and wider tires around everywhere she went? That should have been alarming.

But it wasn't. Sandy, regardless of the cheater slicks Shawn was installing, was still a girl. I had the obvious advantage of biology, a huge advantage in cubic inches, and I assumed a decisive horsepower advantage. I knew her car was a manual transmission car, as was mine, so I had an advantage there as well, because she was a girl. She was likely to miss a gear and cry. I had been racing all over Creek County and Tulsa as well, so I knew I had the edge on her in experience. Sandy had her own pit crew in her brother, but so did I in Tommy, who at that moment was drinking a can of Budweiser that he'd left in his car all day and eating a sleeve of Dolly Madison powdered donuts. My pit crew didn't have any tools or jacks or tires, but it didn't matter. Sandy was a girl. This would be easy. I'd handily put Sandy in her place, squelch the talk of her car, and the world would once again be rotating on its proper axis.

I drove out to the makeshift drag strip on nearly abandoned Slick Road, where we had marked off a start line and an end line a quarter mile down the road in fluorescent orange paint. I beat Sandy there and had to wait for her while she did whatever it was she was doing to her car. My pit crew finished his donuts and had moved on to a week old open bag of Cheetos he'd found in one of my rear floor pans.

When she finally arrived, we lined up, with Tommy serving as the starter, a mixture of powdered sugar and orange Cheeto-dust ringing his mouth. Quite a crowd had gathered as well, as few wanted to miss this epic clash of classic American muscle cars, the two most legendary cars in the county in 1990. A 1968 Road Runner, 440 snarling under a hood vibrating violently from the engine's torque, and a rumbling but unsightly 1970 SS Camaro line up was truly something from another era. Spectators lined the first couple hundred yards of the road, waiting patiently for Tommy to drop his hands.

When he did, both cars angrily roared to life. Sandy's cheater slicks dug in, but the low gearing of my Plymouth allowed me to get her off the line, despite some wheel spin from my narrow bias ply tires. I glanced down to make sure I didn't miss second, and when I glanced up, all I saw was two sets of rapidly disappearing round taillights in the gathering gloom of the early spring evening. As I remember it, Sandy was turning her car around as I crossed that distant orange line, and I passed her coming the other way. She shot me the finger as we passed. I turned around to head back – a proper race was best two out of three – and idled along the road and through the jeering crowd that I can only assume was helpfully trying to motivate me by pointedly reminding me I'd just been beaten – badly - by a girl. As if I, Manhood's Champion, wasn't aware of that. I headed back to the line; I sure wasn't going to take that from a girl.

Sandy was already at the line. I sidled up to her, on the opposite side of the road from the first race. How did Sandy know that was proper protocol? Tommy guided me to the line, and I glanced at her over her misaligned doors. She glared back at me. What was she so angry about?

Tommy dropped his arms, and that, for me, was the high point of the race. Sandy had apparently had a terrible run the first heat, as she destroyed me off the line. In fairness, she did have a significant weight advantage due to the gaping rust holes in her quarter panels. The last thing I saw of Sandy was her deftly rowing through the gears of her four-speed, as no man I knew could do.

Knowing I'd lost the race, I tried to at least make it respectable as I stuck it into third. My old shifter was a lot like trying to shift gears with a rope. I missed the gear. Sandy stabbed her Camaro into third, and off she went, like she had rockets in her twin tailpipes. I was reasonably sure she'd sucked the headlamps out of my Plymouth.

I should have just kept driving past the finish toward wherever Slick Road went, but, humiliated, I made the return trip down the road to congratulate Sandy, but she was gone. She had vanquished me and didn't have any need to speak to me. She knew who was king, er, queen, of Creek County street racing. Muttering excuses to the dispersing-but-still-jeering crowd, I commanded Tommy to get in the car. Popping open another warm beer, he looked over at me with genuine sympathy and white lips. "JEEE- sus Christ, Clay," he said in bewilderment. I told him to shut up. I drove him home in silence.

I later learned that, having such a lead, Sandy had shut her car down well before the finish line. That didn't help salve my bruised ego. I never raced Sandy again, but I sure took out my frustration on the stupid-but-always-game Eric Stubblefield. I am not sure I even saw her car again. Or I may have avoided looking at it. That race may not have been Billie Jean King beating Bobby Riggs, but I learned a very valuable lesson in Girl Power that day.

It was only later that it dawned on me that my mom had been driving a manual transmission pickup for years. Obviously, Eric Stubblefield wasn't the only slow study in Kellyville.

Home

Johnna Kaye and Kevin McCarthy

The majestic walls of the Rocky Mountains grew taller around me like the hug of a childhood blanket. I pushed my weary legs forward through the brambles of the valley floor, numb to the cold and pain of frostbite. I smiled, knowing I'd be adding more scars from younger days to my adult shins.

The sharp tang of smoke in my nose sparked me forward for I knew I was getting close. To what exactly, I didn't know, but I trudged on nevertheless. It'd been too long since I'd seen them. Would they even recognize me now? Would they even be there? There were so many thoughts whirling around in my head, but I refused to let them linger.

A snowflake drifted gently down before me, a talisman to my return. Winter had always been special to us, at least it seemed that way in my memories. Winter had been the season when we'd had time for stories, music, games, talking....

A crow cawed in the distance as if cracking a whip to hurry me on. It would be colder tonight at such an altitude. I had to get there before dark fell.

I passed over the hill and there it was—the four walls of the home most people would call a shanty. To me, it was a palace—a resort for my soul, for this was where my life began. These old worn-out walls held the most precious memories of my youth—a time of happiness and innocence—a time before the war.

I rushed toward the doorway, desperate for the long-awaited touch of my mother's hand, and my little brother, clinging to my leg—though he wouldn't be so young now, would he? I could almost smell the roasted duck, and the thought beckoned my exhausted feet onward—that juicy tender meat that my mother alone knew how to cook to perfection. *Would there be dessert tonight?* I hastened to my long-awaited oasis.

How many years of misery and death of friends and foes had it been? Too many to count, for the truth was too painful to think about. But finally, life would be better. *Oh, how excited they'll be to see me.*

I froze, just outside. I could hear no one. The wind in the distant trees was the only sound to reach my ears. A chill seeped under my skin, and I called, "Ma! Billy! It's me! I'm home! Anyone?" Only silence answered my call and the ghost of my father which we also called the distant wind in the trees.

Frantic, I ran inside. The door swung easily, then fell from my hand. It hit the brittle wooden floor with an ear-piercing crash onto shattered dishes in what was once my sanctuary. I spun in the center of the two-roomed house, for the first time noticing through tunnel-vision the decaying emptiness. That same black crow cawed again in the sky above my head as if in ridicule for not having noticed until now that the roof was not there. The duck, the welcoming arms, the warm fire, all of those were no more than a child's memory of a life that was no more.

What Next?

Kaylene Dow

Hair tangled, face painted, clothes torn, his eyes met hers as the screen door slammed shut. Katy stood frozen on the back step. Alone in the July heat, the man's stare sent a chill down her spine. Katy's plan to play in the back yard was quickly abandoned.

Safely inside with the door locked, Katy crouched down and peered through the curtains, watching until he walked away. Who was he, and what had he been doing out there in the alley? Still shaken, Katy thought about going upstairs and telling her mother. No, Momma would just say she was imagining things or that she was just making it up trying to get attention. Why Momma insisted on saying such things lately, she didn't know; she was not jealous of the baby. Katy sat a little longer on the floor before running back to her room.

Zan was waiting for Katy at the end of the driveway. "What took you so long?"

Katy didn't want to talk about it. "Nothing," she responded. "Just didn't get to leave like I wanted."

That much was true. She would have left sooner, but she kept seeing that face everywhere she looked. She couldn't get him out of her mind. Not wanting to answer any more questions, Katy challenged Zan to a race downtown. Zan won.

Katy told herself to forget about earlier and think about winning the contest. Katy was relieved she had decorated her bike the evening before, or she would not have been ready. The bikes were supposed to gather at the south end of Main Street. Zan's bike looked good, but Katy thought her own might be a little better. *Besides,* she thought confidently, *everyone likes red, white and blue.*

Katy scanned the crowd trying to see if she could spot Curtis Bailey, but he was nowhere to be seen. Maybe he got grounded or something. The thought cheered Katy a bit. Curtis wasn't a real bully or anything, just an annoying neighbor who bragged about something every time she saw him. His skates were newer, his kite flew higher, his bike was faster, blah, blah, blah. The prize would be nice, but beating Curtis Bailey would be even nicer.

Katy took the number from the judge and slipped it over her handle bars. The bikes were to wait until the mayor's black convertible went by and then follow along behind him. Katy hoped she and Zan would be able to ride side by side, but if Curtis showed up, it might be hard to do. Katy was pretty sure he had a crush on Zan, another reason to beat him.

The asphalt was already sticky. Katy sure wished she hadn't been in such a hurry and forgotten the water bottle. After what seemed like hours, they finally saw the mayor's car. Katy and Zan started off at the same speed, but before they reached the bank at the end of the block, Katy found herself behind a group of boys who refused to let her pass them. There was no way to catch Zan. Tired and hot, Katy pedaled alone and told herself it didn't matter. The prize was for decoration anyway, not speed, and the winner wouldn't be announced until later that evening.

The group of bikes followed the mayor around the final corner, ending their journey at Tucker's Grocery. Zan's grandmother had given her a dollar, so that she and Katy could get something cold to drink when they were finished. They each got a grape soda and sat down on the curb.

"I didn't see Curtis anywhere, did you?" asked Zan.

"No. At least that's one good thing that's happened today."

"What do you mean?" Zan set down her soda bottle, and Katy mustered up enough courage and told her about the man. "Sure hope I never see him again. Do you suppose he's left town by now?"

"Maybe," answered Zan. That was not what Katy wanted to hear. She had hoped Zan had some explanation or knew something that would make her feel better, but she had neither. After finishing their drinks, discussing what clothes they would wear and deciding where to meet later, Katy and Zan each headed home.

Momma decided she needed to stay home with the baby. Katy and her dad would be the only ones going, and that suited Katy just fine. Daddy said he would drive Katy and put her bike in the back of the truck, so it wouldn't get messed up. Katy was relieved she wouldn't be riding her bike home in the dark. As soon as supper was over, they loaded up and headed out.

Katy's dad gave her money for a snack and went to find a place to sit. She put her kickstand down and then searched the crowd for Zan. She could see several kids with their bikes, but not Zan. They were both supposed to wear red. Katy suggested red, knowing she would match her bike if she happened to win. A good ten minutes went by before the crowd cleared, and she spotted them, Zan and Curtis Bailey.

The music was loud, and the air smelled of dirt. Katy tried to ignore the fact that they had shown up together and only spoke to Zan.

"I got here early to save you a spot. Curtis stopped me. He didn't enter a bike this year and offered to help me with mine." *Of course, he did,* thought Katy. Determined not to let Curtis make this the worst day ever, Katy got back on her bike and waited for the gate to open. Zan put her bike next to Katy's but stood talking to Curtis until the announcer addressed the crowd. The prize for the best bike was five dollars, and Katy thought five dollars sure would be nice right about now.

At the signal, the gate opened, and all the bike riders entered the arena and circled until they came to the red and blue barrels. Curtis had followed them in and had managed to get between her and Zan.

"I think your bike's going to win," said Curtis with his back to Katy. A pang of guilt hit Katy; to beat Curtis, she realized she needed to beat Zan. Ugh. What next?

Finally, the music ended, and the announcer took out an envelope. The wait was nearly over. Katy held her breath. "Best Decorated Bike goes to--number eighteen." Katy could hardly believe it. She had won! Zan and Curtis congratulated her, and everyone cheered. Katy waved wildly at the crowd. The day was ending a whole lot better than it started. Smiling as she turned back around, the announcer pointed to one of the barrels, and much to Katy's dismay, there he was, hair tangled, face painted, clothes torn, and holding up her five dollars, the rodeo clown.

Go, Green

Andrea Foster

Gloriana Nesta sat in the bleachers scanning the crowd with her binoculars. She had to find the persons who had eaten the brownies. She hadn't known that Lil Freddy had put something in the batter that morning. She'd had no idea.

She had proudly baked her special recipe brownies and carted them off to the bake sale at the ball game that afternoon. She was so excited that they had sold out in the first ten minutes. That was when her teenage son Freddy had come up to the table, grinning and giggling.

"They sold out, huh?" He questioned with a smirk on his face.

"Yes, they sure did! I bet that they'll ask me to repeat that recipe again."

"I bet they will!" Freddy laughed behind his cupped hand. "…especially after I put that green stuff in there!"

"What green stuff?" Gloriana felt her stomach drop, and her face twisted as the horror sunk in. Freddy had put something in the brownies. "What did you put in there? Freddy, how could you?!"

"Some green stuff I found. Looked kinda like leaves—green—you know. I ground it up and put it into the batter and mixed it up and then put it in the oven like you said."

Oh, dear, Gloriana was beginning to freak out. She had asked her son to take the batter, scoop it into the baking dish, and pop it in the oven while she took a shower to get ready. Now, what?!

"Freddy! How could you!? We could be arrested! Where did you get it? Why did you do that? You could go to jail! I could go to jail! Oh my gosh!"

She hadn't waited to hear his reply. She left him there in the parking lot and ran to the field and up onto the bleachers and started scouring the crowd with binoculars.

She saw the McGinty twins acting crazy, but they were always unruly and silly. Did it look like they were laughing more than usual?

She saw Johnny Carmichael scarfing down pizza like a pro. Was he eating more than usual? Did he look famished, more than usual?

She saw a group of girls giggling at the boys and eating brownies. Her heart jumped. She ran over to them, leaping over bleacher seats, making the bleachers bounce like a trampoline.

"Hey!" Other folks were not so happy about this jostling.

Breathless, Gloriana ran over to the girls, knocking her brownies out of their hands.

"Mrs. Nesta! What are you doing?!"

Gloriana looked horrified, but they looked even more so, that Freddy's mother was acting all crazy.

"Mom! Mom! Mom!" Here came Freddy, grinning his head off, and shouting at her. "Mom! Stop!"

"What do you mean, stop?" shouted his mother. "I

have to stop them! We can't allow them to eat those brownies! Who knows what will happen?!"

"Mom! Mom! Stop! Nothing will happen. They will just feel better."

"I'm sure they will, young man!"

"Mom, Mom," Freddy was falling over, laughing so hard that he was doubling over.

The teenage girls were standing still, with shocked looks on their faces. They had no idea what to make of this.

"Mom, I put spinach in there. The green stuff was spinach."

"Spinach!?" Gloriana stopped dead in her tracks, stunned.

"Yeah, Mom, I heard from that cookbook by the comedian's wife that you could add good things to bad things and at least get some nutrition. So I decided to add spinach and see if anybody noticed. I guess not!" He kept covering his huge smile with his cupped hand.

"Freddy!" Gloriana just stared. What a crazy woman he had caused her to become. She reached into her pocket and handed her son $20. "Okay, Freddy, now go buy these young ladies something else to eat. Something without spinach! Girls, I owe you some brownies." They all burst out laughing.

Painting with Mel Tillis

Debbie Fogle

"Don't make plans for this weekend. We are painting the entire front room." In August of 1978, my mother yelled out this command from the kitchen. Now, my mother is only five foot-two inches in height, but you NEVER disobey a request from mom. The plan began to paint the front room over the weekend. I didn't know one thing about painting.

I asked to make a call to my friend Kelley. Kelley is the best friend that everyone dreams of, because she totally understands a mother's demand. Her mother and my mother had that true quality of love and understanding, and we knew the consequences if we disobeyed. Kelley was sad I couldn't go to Rollerrama with her, but being the cool friend she is, she volunteered to come over and help out. I suggested, no. Helping with my mother is one thing, but my step-father was also going to be home. He would be giving the painting instructions.

My step father is a blend of *Fonzie* from *Happy Days* and *Red Forman* from *The 70's Show*. That is how it was in my house growing up. The household with three girls and one boy. My littlest sister was too young to help, but that didn't mean she didn't try to assist with the painting task. My brother was bummed because he was there and not out cruising around for girls. My mother announced at dinner on Friday night that we would begin painting at nine o'clock Saturday morning.

"WHAT! No sleeping in?" was my outburst. The moment I viewed my mother's eyes, I knew I needed to eat my dinner and hush up.

Saturday morning, it began. Plastic tarps and old sheets covered the furniture, and we tried to cover the floor but ran out of tarps. The buckets of paint miraculously appeared. Being a teenager, I don't know how three cans of paint arrived at our house. My mother was the catalog queen of our neighborhood. She didn't drive a car, so she ordered a lot through the mail. Did she order the paint? The fact was: the paint was ready to be applied to the starving walls and ceiling.

The moment came when my mother did the greatest stunt ever. She brought out the radio so we could listen to music. Oh, but there was a catch to this treat. The music to be played was what my step-father approved of. "The only radio station to listen to is KUZZ," he declared.

My sister and I gave each other that look of acceptance. We were there, so we better just get the painting done with. Somehow, my brother was able to skip out of the painting job, and we didn't see him until Saturday evening. My brother was almost eighteen years old; he knew how to sneak out of home painting day. My sister and I were not so lucky. Oh, but wait! The story starts here.

Now, every one of us wore prescription eye glasses. And did we think to remove our glasses while we were painting? NO! Did we think of changing into some old clothing before we started painting? Well, my step-father had his work clothes on. You can say my mother was focused on getting the painting done, not on our clothing choices.

The duty of painting the ceiling was given to me. Oh, I didn't think it was an honor, the way my sister made it out to be. I received this glorified duty of ceiling painting, because I was five foot eight inches high in my stocking feet.

"Debbie doesn't need to use the ladder," chirped my cute little sister. So, there I was, rolling the paint all along the ceiling. Thank goodness, it wasn't that weird bumpy ceiling. All the while, the radio was blasting out the latest country music tunes.

Then something strange happened. Around four o'clock in the afternoon, my parents were different. They were laughing and giggling. My step-father applied some paint on a paint roller and proceeded to apply a layer of paint to my mother's backside. I froze and viewed my escape route from the front room. My mother began laughing and giggling, and my step-father joined in the laughter. My sister and I looked at each other and soon began laughing as well. Then the moment came: *Mel Tillis's* song, *Coca-Cola Cowboy* came on the radio.

I grabbed one of the rollers and applied paint to the rhythm of the song. I hooked one finger in a belt loop on my ditto pants and began dancing a funny cowboy dance. My sister was looking at me as if I was crazy. My mother began doing her cool jive dance that she always does, and my step-father was looking at us, like we were crazy. Soon, we were all doing crazy dance moves as we finished up painting the front room.

What a glorious moment to share with my family, only to find out we couldn't get the paint off our prescription glasses.

We all had to get new glasses the next week. The paint didn't wash out of our clothing the way it washed off the brushes and rollers. Oopsie on that too.

My step-father would point out every now and then, "I think you missed a spot over there on the ceiling."

No one else painted the ceiling, so of course the blame would go to me for the shades of white and off-white in the one corner where I began my *Coca-Cola Cowboy* dance. Even when we moved out of that house three years later, the missed area was never painted.

We all have those memories of painting a room or a house, and something so funny happens that you can no longer paint. Another time, my sister stepped into a roll pan that my mom just filled with paint. It just seems something has to happen when my family is painting a house.

I am still assigned to paint the ceiling, only now I wear the designated painting goggles and clothing, and after three apartments and three houses, I feel I have perfected the technique of house painting, but every time I begin to paint, I remember listening to Mel Tillis singing *Coca-Cola Cowboy* on the radio.

The Perils of Growing up Shy, Skinny, Weak, and a Boy with an Odd Name

Alton "Tuna" Dobbins

Bullies and girls.
Bullies first, then girls.

Have you ever been bullied? Most of you can say yes. Some of you can say no and mean it. I'm not one of those. As a shy, skinny kid with an odd name, I got bullied in school. It didn't help that my light skin turned beet red when I was embarrassed. My classmates seemed to enjoy embarrassing me and watching me turn red.

Most bullies don't beat you up and take your lunch money. Most bullying comes from classmates, and most of them don't think that what they are doing is actually bullying. The embarrassment they cause is just having a little fun to them. Some bullies were a little more serious, and they seemed to delight in making another hurt. These were the worst.

School bullies pick on the kids that are different, and it doesn't take much difference to attract their attention. A different race, a different accent, being shy, being a loner, being skinny and weak, you name it. If you're different in some way or can be made to look different, you're a target.

It doesn't help having an unusual name either. My father picked out my name because he refused to let my mother call me "Kirby." All things considered, I am glad to have the name my father gave me instead of Kirby. Still, John, Bill, Bob, or Joey would have been better in elementary school, especially since my mother insisted that everyone use my whole first name when addressing and not shorten it. She insisted that she didn't like nicknames for her children and didn't want others shortening my name to just "Al."

Looking back on this, I find it really odd that my mother would do this, because she grew up in a family of nine, and every one of her brothers and sisters had a nickname, including her. Maybe that was her way of rebelling against nicknames, because of the way they were used in her family.

Somehow, my mother's desire to avoid nicknames didn't seem to apply to my sister. Dad started calling her "Skeeter" when she was young, and it stuck. Even my mother called her Skeeter every now and then. My brother and I always got our full first name used.

Back to bullies. Bullies intimidate you, embarrass you and generally make you look stupid or sad. Elementary school seems to be a haven for bullies – boys and girls. Boys pick on boys, and girls pick on girls. I was a boy, so the other boys picked on me. The first real bullying started in fourth grade. Not my first fourth grade school but my second. I started fourth grade in that same school that I had attended second and third grade, but my family moved in the middle of the school year. I didn't know anyone at the new school. That meant that I was automatically different.

My first fourth grade school was hard to leave, because I loved the fourth grade teacher there. I even had the fantasy that I would marry her someday. It didn't occur to me at the time that she was probably already married since we called her "Mrs. Gunther." When I got to my new school, I didn't like my new teacher, and I don't remember her name. I also quickly learned that I was behind the kids in this new school. My old school was teaching at a lower level, so I was behind all the new kids.

No friends, stupid, and an odd name. Boy, was I a target. My new school was teaching fractions in math class, and I didn't have a clue what they were. I failed my first math test the first week I was there, and I wasn't much better in the other subjects. I was embarrassed in the worst way. I was trying to pay attention in class and I thought I was catching on to fractions, but when that first test came, I got most of the fraction problems wrong. Simple enough, I thought. If 1 over 1 (1/1) = 1 then 2 over 2 (2/2) must be equal to 2. The test went downhill from there.

The other students noticed my test score and made fun of me. Of course, I turned red as a beet. Before changing schools, I thought I was good in math. I had a lot of catching up to do, and I was going to do it all on my own. I was not about to ask anyone for help and be embarrassed over and over again. I had always been a loner, learning or playing by myself, because my brother and sister were much older than me and didn't spend time with me. My mother was always busy keeping the house going, so I spent a lot of time alone. I studied twice as much to catch up.

Over the next few weeks, my math test scores improved but I was still at the bottom of the class. By the end of that school year, I was making some of the highest grades in math and making the other students look bad. But I'm still the odd boy out and the bullies in school don't like being shown up by a skinny nerd that can't play sports. Physical fitness was not my strong suit, and that played a big hand in my not being any good at sports. Years later, I learned that I was very well coordinated when it came to driving cars and flying jets, but that's another story.

Back to school sports: I couldn't catch a baseball or hit the damn thing. I could throw it pretty accurately but not as far as others. As a pitcher, I needed to do all the other things well too. When teams were selected, I was one of the last picked. Football was out of the question also since I was so skinny and relatively weak.

So, my bullying problems started in fourth grade and continued through sixth grade. One time, I decided to stand up to a bully in my fourth grade year. He "invited" me to meet him after school. I knew better than to run for home, but I didn't know how to fight either. One punch, and I was down. I didn't even get a shot in before it was over. Big time embarrassment and I tried to hide the next couple of weeks hoping everyone would forget. Kids don't forget that sort of stuff, and other bullies started picking on me.

For the next couple of years, I tried to avoid every known bully, but I couldn't always do that. It seemed that every week, I'd get embarrassed by a bully. I just wanted to hide or not go to school. The loner in me wanted to be that way again. When you're the target of the school bullies, you don't make friends either. No one in the school wants to be friends with a target.

My older brother wasn't around to defend me either. He was four years older than me, so he was always in a different school when we were growing up. He didn't like me much back then anyway. He got stuck "babysitting" me when he would rather hang with his friends and do stuff teens were doing. I was nothing but a problem for him.

My father figured out what was going on, but he also knew that I needed to sort this out, or I'd be putting up with bullies the rest of my life. My father was never much of a talker, but when he said something, it was important to remember what he said. He reminded me that I needed to learn how to deal with bullies in school, because they were everywhere. I don't think he expected me to handle the bullies the way I did. If he did, he probably would have cautioned me to try a different way.

I lived through the sixth grade, but I knew something had to change when I went to junior high school. Just like changing schools in fourth grade, there would be plenty of new kids to get to know and plenty of kids from the old school that went to a different junior high school. So, everyone would be in a new situation and trying to make new friends. This could be both good and bad; it just depended on how I handled it. I knew a few of my sixth grade antagonists would be joining me at the new school.

So, over the summer between sixth and seventh grade, I started carrying a pocket knife. Pocket knives are real handy tools and can be used for many things. I also realized that my pocket knife might be just the thing I needed to even things up with a few of the bullies. The pocket knife my dad gave me was a little two-bladed thing, and the large blade was hard to open. The retainer spring was pretty strong. I knew if it were to be used in self-defense, I'd need to be able to get it open faster. There were plenty of tools around the house, (my dad was an auto mechanic) so I started working on my knife. A little filing here and bending there and I could get that long blade out by just sliding my thumb across the knife. The blade would flip right out. I practiced this a lot. When I went to junior high school in the fall, I'd be ready, and I'd stand my ground against any bully that got in my face. One way or the other, win or lose, I was going to fight back.

Back in the 1960's, carrying a knife to school wasn't a problem. In fact, it wasn't unusual at all to see all sorts of weapons around every school. At junior high school, a few of the pickup trucks in the faculty parking lot would have rifles or shotguns hanging in the rear window. By the time I got to high school, both students and teachers had rifles or shotguns displayed in their pickup trucks. Sometimes both would be in the parking lot comparing their weapons. Pocket knives were everywhere.

That first month at junior high school, a bully I knew from sixth grade decided to take up where he left off and got in my face on the playground. He probably wanted to make his mark on the new school as soon as possible, and he assumed that I would be an easy target to establish his reputation.

He didn't expect me to behave any differently than before, so he was really surprised when I pushed him back against the fence hard and rammed my left forearm under his chin and pressed it against his throat. Before he knew it, I had pulled my knife from my pocket and flipped the blade open with my right thumb.

Luckily for him (and me), I still had my thumb on the blade when I pushed it into his belly. Only about a quarter of an inch of blade managed to penetrate his shirt and skin. If I had stabbed him deeper, I'd have been in detention the rest of the year, or worse. He screamed like a little girl. I told him to leave me alone and never touch me again. Then I let him go. He ran as fast as he could to get away from me.

I'm sure I was shaking at the time, but I can't remember now. I know it felt good, though, because I was watching "him," the bully, run away from "me," the skinny weakling.

I never heard a word from him or anybody else about the incident, and I never pulled my knife in anger again. As it turned out, I never needed to. The rest of junior and high school, I didn't back down from bullies, either. While I was still the skinny, weakling in the school, the school bullies picked on others that were less likely to pull a knife on them. Most bullies are cowards and fold like a cheap suit when actually confronted. The ones at my junior high were no different.

These days, you will need a different way to confront bullies. Finding and making friends in new places is the first thing to do. Don't try to go it alone. Bring teachers and other adults into the picture and let them help you out.

As I progressed through junior high school, bullies stopped being a concern for me. I think, maybe, they were scared of me now. The next big problem for me turned out to be girls.

I was starting to break the loner mold by making new friends in junior high school and started noticing girls. I was still shy around girls and easily embarrassed when they were around. You might think that since I had an older sister, that wouldn't be true but it was. When I was growing up, I didn't talk to my sister much. She was six years older than me and in a whole different world. We didn't share a thing in common. Oh, I wanted to get to know girls better, but I just didn't know how. I didn't realize it at the time that all I needed to do was be myself and be friendly, and they would be friendly back.

So, small talk with a girl was impossible, and if I found myself saying or doing something stupid, I'd get embarrassed, and I'd avoid talking to that girl again. For me, girls became the new bullies. Not that any of them went out of the way to hurt me, it just happened, and it was usually my fault. If I embarrassed myself around a girl, she would tell her friends, and all the girls would have a good laugh about me.

Figuring out how to confront this new set of troubles was going to take a lot longer, and I couldn't use my knife.

You want to scare away bullies, but girls, you want to keep around and get to know. How do I do that and not look stupid or embarrass myself? Part of my problem was that I was very conscious of the fact that I was poor. My allowance was very small, so I didn't have money to buy a girl a soda or take one out on a real date. That made me very reluctant to ask a girl out, and that just made my problems last longer.

I had the idea that a first date ought to be something special, but how do you get to that first date with a girl if you can't even make small talk with them and become friends first? It took me a long time to figure that out. After I got my driver's license, my father provided me with a car. Just having a car in high school was impressive, but very few of my classmates knew that I rarely had any money left over after buying gas for that old car.

Needless to say, I rarely dated in high school or college. One date, one embarrassment and that was it. I'd wait for the next chance with a girl that didn't know me and hope to do better. Of course, that didn't work either. I asked a girl to the senior prom, and she accepted. We had our picture made at the entrance, and that was about the most fun we had that evening. I couldn't dance (still don't like to dance) and I stepped on her feet too many times. We didn't have anything in common, so we didn't talk much either. I'm sure she was relieved when I took her home.

I wasn't any better in college, either, but somewhere along the way I must have decided to just be me and let the chips fall where they may with girls. Girls started to like me and finally love me. I figured out who I am and what I am, and I decided that I'm not a bad guy. Oh, I still have a few things to work on but, overall, I'm okay. My wife must think so because we've been together nineteen years and she still loves me.

Oh, Those Sweet Oranges

Rosemarie Durgin

Mother and I were still living in Bamberg, in northern Bavaria of Western Germany. We no longer lived up in the cold little attic room. We had moved to the ground floor. It was a large room, with a *Kacheloven,* a large tile ornamented heater, and there was a very large window, looking out to the street. We even had access to a kitchen across the hall, and the bathroom was just down a few steps from the apartment door.

I was happy in that room. The best part of the new living space was the other member of the apartment. Mr. Heldt, was blind, middle aged. I was awed by him. He got about his part of the apartment as if he was sighted. I tried closing my eyes, walking around in the dark, and of course, I bumped into doors and walls and furniture. But what surprised me the most was that he had books he could read, without eyes. He had all the classics in Braille.

I could not read yet at all, and here he was reading with his fingers. I looked at those huge books with the thick, beige pages and little bumps and holes punched into them. What was most amazing was that Mr. Heldt was able to teach me how to read. That was the time I was home from school with the mumps. Mother had to go to work, and I could not manage to put two letters together to produce the word *so.* No, I could not say *so.* I had no problem with longer words, but *so* was my stumbling block. Mr. Heldt was finally able to get me to put the two letters together and pronounce the word.

This particular day, my friend Erika, who lived two floors above us, came running to us all excited to tell us the little green-grocer up the street was selling wonderful huge oranges. I had to ask her what oranges are. I had never seen or tasted one. When she told my mother and showed her the fruit she had bought, mother became excited and sent me to that little shop.

We were able to purchase twelve of the orange globes. We were so surprised that we were able to get so much fruit without the expenditure of food ration stamps. I ran up the street as fast as my seven-year-old legs would carry me. Once home again, my mother was so pleased with me, she explained how juicy and sweet oranges are, and it seemed that these particular oranges were what she called blood oranges from Spain, the sweetest kind. She told me we would have to share them for as long as possible. We would have one orange between us once a day.

I could hardly wait for her to peel that first orange. I was salivating. Then, Mother gave me the first little section. I bit into it, expecting this most juicy sweet morsel. It was juicy, but oh so bitter.

"Muttie, this does not taste sweet. It is bitter." My mom took a bite and almost spit it out.

"I don't know what is wrong with this. Surely, they don't sell spoiled fruit. We have to eat them." She declared. "We need the vitamin C, and we don't have the money to waste. We just have to eat those oranges."

For years after that I would not eat oranges; that bitter taste stayed in my mind. Finally, many years later, I was given an orange to eat, and in order to be polite, I ate the thing, girding myself for the bitter taste. Was I ever surprised that the orange was sweet and juicy and luscious!

After that, oranges became my favorite fruit. I just could not understand what was wrong with those oranges I had bought in Bamberg.

Many years later, (I was married by then) my friend Pat invited me upstairs to have breakfast with her. She had fruit that looked much like those oranges we had in Bamberg, pale orange with little red splotches in the fruit. Pat cut the fruit in half, and topped it with brown sugar, and heated it for a few minutes in the oven. (We did not have microwaves ovens back then.) To my surprise, it tasted good, but still with that same bitter taste.

"What kind of oranges are these? They taste a bit bitter."

"Oh, those are not oranges at all. They are grapefruits. Have you never eaten them?"

"No, I don't think so, but wait, yes, perhaps once, a long time ago. We thought the fruit was bad."

I had no idea what a grapefruit was. I ran downstairs to get my dictionary. It had no word for grapefruit in the German section, no translation at all. A few years later, I obtained a newer dictionary. There was a translation for grapefruit: *pampelmuse.* I had never heard that word.

Neither my mother nor my friends were familiar with that fruit. I will have a grapefruit once in a great while now, but I do not like them; that first experience is what has stayed with me all these years.

I Recall Fondly

Julie Marquardt

I love writing haiku poems. For those unfamiliar with haiku, allow me to enlighten you. Haiku is a three line Japanese poem comprised of just seventeen syllables. Five syllables make up the top and bottom lines and the middle line has seven syllables. Like this:

Counting syllables,
Top and bottom lines have five,
Middle line, seven.

Traditionally these poems are one stanza in length and reflect thoughts about the natural world. I break from tradition by writing haiku about anything and everything, so they are almost always more than one stanza, and they tell a story. Here's my story:

Thoughts of yesterday,
Come into my mind often,
Childhood memories

Not an only child,
Brother and sister, one each,
They are my best buds

Pa was a farm boy,
Met a would be school teacher,
It all started then

Soon a baby came,
A boy with blonde hair, blue eyes,
Four years later… me

Then another girl,
Baby sister won my heart,
With her big brown eyes

We were Navy brats,
When Pa got the call to serve,
So, off we all went

We stuck together,
Home's where the family was,
No matter what place

In Twentynine Palms,
Running down the dunes to home,
Hot sand fills our shoes

Minneapolis,
Nice in summer, but winter-
Snowy, bitter cold

Loved San Diego,
Barbie dolls, jacks and the beach,
Playing in the sun

At ten, new orders,
The island, Okinawa,
Not far from Japan

My favorite place,
What freedom and fun we had,
I recall fondly

See us together,
Good times as a family,
A great place to live

Piecing memories,
Places we went, things we did,
It still makes me smile

"Let's go for a ride",
Should be family motto,
See what we can see

Tiered, green rice paddies,
Bent in ankle deep water,
Tending all by hand

Thatched roofed villages,
People wearing wooden shoes,
And kimonos, too

Cars could not go fast,
Top speed limit was thirty,
But we all felt safe

Once in a while, though,
On an abandoned air strip,
We'd fly at fifty!

It felt dangerous,
Like we were flying through air,
We'd all shout and laugh

Exploring the beach,
Played in the East China Sea,
Looked for hermit crabs

Searching in tide pools,
To find baby octopus,
Hiding in coral

If we were lucky,
We would see it squirt black ink
Clouding the water

One day in the sea,
Saw Pa running near the shore,
Sea snake chasing him!

Hide and Seek, or War,
Watch out for the habu snakes,
Hiding in tall grass

Scattered through the hills,
Climbing on turtle-backed tombs,
No disrespect meant

Six inch centipedes,
One crawled up my dad's pant leg,
Should have seen him dance!

Shopping with Mama,
People loved to touch my hair,
Long, fine, white-blonde silk

Wanting to buy it,
Some offered to cut it then,
Politely said no

Went to Girl Scout camp,
Where we bunked in canvas tents,
Military style

I traded lunches,
With Okinawan Girl Scout,
Feared getting her bag

Not adventurous,
Eating the different food,
Seaweed is not food!

Saw Hello Dolly!
Mary Martin live on stage,
Singing and dancing!

It was magical,
There was such movement and sound,
Could not stop smiling

I envied those folk,
Twirling and jumping around,
What a job to have!

The Beatles came out,
Oh, my, look at that long hair,
Adults shake their heads

No TV 'til four,
Unless a typhoon was near,
Then TV all day!

Beach Blanket Bingo,
Girls wore 'racy' bikinis,
Annette and Frankie

In between the fun,
Not all of life was roses,
There was sadness, too

The Vietnam War.
We were much closer to it,
Than a lot of folks

Hush, hush troop movement,
We knew it was going on,
But no talking, please

Don't remember fear,
I was just a child then, and…
My father was safe

We heard the sad news,
President Kennedy killed,
The world is in shock

Grown-ups want to know,
What is this world coming to?
There is no answer

I see myself then,
White blonde hair and deep blue eyes,
So different now

It's funny sometimes,
Seeing my siblings faces,
Staring back at me

Who are these people?
Don't recognize the old folks,
Not like in my mind

In my mind, we're young,
Wrinkle free and blonde headed,
Few cares in the world

Where have the years gone?
How can time pass so quickly?
It seems to fly by

When I remember,
Grateful for my memories,
They're what make me... me.

The Collector

Karen Bullock

My father was a collector. He collected things, all sorts of things. As a child, I remember a large gunny sack of marbles of all sizes and colors. Dad would take one out, and there would be a story about that particular marble, back into the sack, another marble, and another tale. It was if he had a personal relationship with each marble in that sack, which he did. But marbles were not his only collection.

Large metal sculptures decorated every yard of every house in which we lived; farm implements, tools of various sizes and functions laid about, monumental stacks of lumber littered our fields. A pair of pliers and a set of post hole diggers might adorn the wire fence while a concrete finishing machine, long past its prime, cluttered the drive way or pasture, and an old Dazey butter churn sat waiting on the porch. It had been waiting for years. An empty cable spool became a table in the backyard, so one could sit on summer nights and talk, eat or just watch the sun go down.

It was a multi-purpose table: tea glasses sat on it; backyard dinners graced it; small construction projects were built on it; feet were propped on it; dogs were groomed upon its top.

And there were dogs. Our home was always a

kennel of various breeds, bird dogs, coon dogs, squirrel dogs and just plain dog dogs, dogs of questionable pedigree or heritage, small Chihuahua, monster wolf-like dogs, in addition to the curs and mongrels of all sizes in between.

Some of our pets had bizarre personalities. There was a hunting dog that was gun-shy; a mother dog that nursed, defended and raised several litters of puppies, kittens; and once, even a baby rabbit and a bird dog that ran so far and so often, his feet bled and he had to wear leather dog booties which he chewed off with two bites. We had squirrel dogs that never barked when they treed and coon dogs that yodeled throughout the night.

To compliment the collection of hunting dogs, there were guns - guns of all sizes, calibers and styles; revolvers, shotguns, rifles, muzzle loaders and combinations of each. One story goes that I used a 22 caliber boot-pistol as a teething ring. Dad would proudly display the small pistol bearing the scrapings of my newly-erupting baby teeth on its grips. There were stories about each gun. This one, he dug up in the California desert. This one didn't have a very good safety and caused him to damn-near shoot his dog when out hunting one day. He spent all day one time building new walnut grips for this one. When my father died, he had over fifty different guns.

But my father's best collection was people, not your ordinary run-of-the-mill people, but the people most of society wished gone, orphans, odd-balls, characters, misfits, people on the fringe. These unique individuals inhabited my childhood in the same way other children had

toy cars or dolls. These were the ones Dad collected.
Some, like Bob, a young, slow-talking Georgian, came to
stay.

Bob was my Dad's partner for seven years until one
day, he just up and left without a word or a note. Others
came for coffee and conversation and left only to return
another day. But all had a commonality. They all had a
story. Each, like the marbles, could be pulled out and a
story was told. These people were the people of legends.

There was Dead Eye (who knows what his real
name was, to our clan he was always "Dead Eye"). Dead
Eye lived in the middle of the high desert of California, a
hermit. Since it was ninety miles to the nearest town, he
had to haul water in large metal drums to the two trailer
houses in which he lived. We visited him periodically,
because Dad had leased the rights to harvest cactus from
his land to sell at the nursery he and Mom owed.

Dead Eye was a barrel-chested man who tacked
pictures of himself standing beside large tunas, sail fish
and other ocean fish to the walls of his trailers. Besides
Dad and me, I never knew him to have another visitor or
another friend, but I often wondered why a man who spent
his life on the seas would choose to live out his life as a
hermit on the desert. And I often wondered, too, how did
Dad meet him?

Then there was Gordon and his sidekick "Edgerly",
a little beagle dog that rode on the back of the driver's seat
with Gordon. Gordon was a tall, raw-boned retiree who
had spent his life driving the big trucks. He wore two
hearing aids. Sometimes it was tiring to talk to him,

because you had to holler at the top of your lungs.

Listening to him could be just as tiring, because Gordon spoke at the top of his lungs. His favorite subject was politics. Everything bad in life was blamed on FDR and the Democrats.

Carl Albert, a favorite son of Oklahoma, was the speaker of the house at the time we knew Gordon. House Speaker Albert grew up in a small community just ten miles from the town in which we lived. There may have been stories about his capacity to drink one under the table, or how he was seen walking along the streets of McAlester (our nearest large town), or how at the early age of thirteen, he had told his teacher he wanted to be in congress, but they were good humored stories, tongue-in-cheek stories. No one ever said anything bad about THE SPEAKER. No one, that is, except Gordon.

He called him "That sawed-off, monkey-faced, son-of-a-bitch". Not necessarily what I usually heard about Carl Albert. When Gordon passed away, Edgerly came to live with us, another addition to the kennel. He repaid this kindness by attacking a wounded, rabid skunk and preventing it from biting my Dad. The little hero died quietly and quickly soon afterwards.

"T-Bone" was another member of Dad's collection. He was about the same age as my Dad and had spent most of his life either working construction or making moonshine. He was a good hunting partner who had several large Airedales that used to chase coyotes. But it was his old horse about which the stories were told.

One day "T" came to the house and asked Dad to put

the poor aged beast out of its misery. This horse was a remarkable animal, for back in "T's" moonshining days, this old nag would carry the finished product in fruit jars hung across his back in saddle bags. "He never broke a jar" was the epitaph T would extol. In fact, you could tap two fruit jars together, and I would swear that horse would tippy-toe across the pasture. When T retired from moonshining, the horse was retired to the back pasture to live a more peaceful and more lawful life.

And now, here was T-Bone asking my Dad to do what he couldn't. I never knew if Daddy helped "put him down", but I do know that his carcass wasn't left in the field for coyotes. He was buried six-feet under like any good friend. "He never broke a jar."

Lawson was a plumber. He was a blue-eyed Irishman who was as soft-spoken as Gordon was loud. Normally, he would come over for coffee while he and Dad discussed construction jobs. A walking contradiction, Lawson was a big man whose body belied a gentleness seldom seen in construction workers. The most unusual feature about him was this large tumor that grew from the back of his head right where it attached to his neck. When asked by an inquisitive four-year-old foster child (Oh, yes, Dad collected kids, too!) "What is THAT?" Lawson, unembarrassed, replied, "You see I have more brains than most folks, and my head can't hold them all."

My favorite person in Dad's collection, though, was "Rattlesnake Bill". Rattlesnake did exactly what his name implied; he collected rattlers, either for their skins or for medical research. He was a small man with a shock of coal-black hair who moved in quick, cat-like gestures. I never saw him in anything but bib over-alls. In the winter, he wore a shirt under them, normally plaid; but in the hot summer, he just wore over-alls. He would often visit at the kitchen table (this is where most of the really important conversations happened at our house). Dad and he would talk about hunting and guns and other manly-stuff. Bill would talk about catching snakes and how he would pull the fangs and poke his arms with it to develop an immunity to snake venom. He'd been bitten several times, been in the hospital several times and damn near died several times, but I don't think any of these little mishaps ever caused him to consider a different line of work.

There was one particular visit I will remember the rest of my life. He had come into the kitchen to begin the ritual of polite conversation when he said sitting was hard for him because of his gun. (He never went anywhere without his gun.) Dad told him to just set it on the table next to his cup. From the folds of his overalls, Rattlesnake Bill pulled a pistol that was a sight to behold.

It was a six-shooter with a barrel that seemed to go on forever. I mean, this thing was a foot long if it was an inch, a real hog leg of a pistol. Nothing was ever said about it; he didn't offer to show it around like one normally did with guns. No explanation was asked and none was volunteered. He just set it on the edge of the table, drank his coffee and visited. When conversation lagged, I noticed all of us staring at that gun, but no one ever said anything. It was like we all were trying to pretend there wasn't anything unusual about having a monster revolver lying on our table. When the visit was over, the gun disappeared into the recesses of his over-alls and Bill continued to walk down the road, though somewhat stiff-legged, I might add. I never saw that gun again, but I was always aware that Rattlesnake carried it or one like it. In Bill's line of work, a man couldn't be too careful.

My Dad died many years ago. His collections were cleaned out, divided up among friends and family, or sold, but my memories fill me with a sense of wonderment. It was unthinkable to me all fathers weren't like mine, and it wasn't until I moved out into the "real world" that I discovered my father was unique.

Because of him, I'm different than the run-of-the-mill daughter and because of this difference, I would like to think I would have been a member of Dad's special collection of people, that I would have sat around the table and talked of hunting and guns and the weather while sipping an endless cup of coffee. I would like to think that my idiosyncrasies would have been exaggerated and extolled to other members of the collection. That I am the stuff of legends, like my Dad and his collections.

I miss you, Dad.

The First Memory is the Strongest

Melly Kerfoot

When most people think of their childhood, they remember a time of innocence. Sweet bubblegum memories, even if laced with occasional tears, are the norm. This is how it should be: childhood is a time of learning, and a child's first lessons should be of love and trust. This is the building block of humanity: love and trust first, then the harsh lessons.

Not for me, though. My first lesson was of deceit.

I remember the day so vividly. It was early summer, the sun beating down on my chubby toddler arms and my toes buried into the cool grass. There are less clear memories, vague ideas of my hair pulled back out of my face into tight ponytails, flowers blooming in the nearby flowerbed, animals roaming nearby. Those might be displaced memories, thoughts that you insert into a recollection to fill in the blanks. Everyone does it, especially to the older memories. It helps us feel as if the puzzle has more of its pieces. As if our memories were more like Swiss cheese and less like tiny pockets of color in a grey void. Those aren't the important pieces of this memory though.

The most important pieces are like technicolor in a sea of fuzziness. That's what I remember the most from that day. Slender, iridescent wings attached to a dark elongated body. Twitching, shimmering as it haltingly scaled the edge of a mud patch near my feet. My three year old attention zeroed in on it in fascination: the most beautiful butterfly in existence.

There might have been words that bubbled out of my mouth as I bent to examine it more closely. Gibberish, or maybe I had already gained the skill of language and actually said the word, "butterfly." Most likely, it was somewhere in between as I took only a moment to jump from seeing the shiny creature, to acquiring the shiny creature.

My fist shot out and captured the insect, quick as a thought. I straightened up, my face alight in triumph, when belatedly, the pain began. My hand was on fire. That is too elegant a thought: there was pain, excruciating, the worst I had ever felt. There was no way to calm my thinking enough to find out what the problem was. I could only scream mindlessly, clenching every muscle in my body, until finally my mother found me.

And so when you come at me, with your sweet words, and your gentle touches, and you try to convince me of your benevolence, I am not fooled. Even though I seem to have the same level of naivete as everyone else, I have learned my lesson. I look at you, and I see your sharp, glistening wings. I see your spikey legs and elongated thorax. I can see you are a wasp from here.

And I will crush you just as easily.

An Honorable Dog

Kandy Anderson

My puppy was precious
When she was little

I'd hold her close
And feed her Kibble.

When she was five
She lost a foot

A bear trap or something
I never looked

Dad thought we'd have to put her down
I cried like a baby when he wasn't around

The fault was all mine, I've tried to let it be
If she hadn't tripped that trap, trying to protect me

An honorable dog, I tell you today
Seems like she was here...only yesterday.

Legs and Leeches

Sue D. L. Smith

I remember me and my three sisters going to City Park as children to play with our two cousins (the six of us were all girls) and how fun that was. We would slide down the slide and swing on the swings and go in circles on the merry-go-round. It was so, so nice! There was a fence around the park, so we had a good sense of boundaries. The park was situated on the corner of two streets that intersected, Pipestone and Britain Avenue, in Benton Harbor, Michigan. Traffic passed by the park throughout the day, but we were oblivious to it.

Our identical-twin female cousins (we called them "The Twins") were only four months older than I. I was the second-born girl in my family, and my older sister was about a year and a half older than me. My third-born sister was a year and 8 days younger than me, and my youngest sister was a year and a half younger than the third-born. Due to all six of us being so close in age, we enjoyed playing together. The Twins' actual names were Karen and Kathy. They were a bit more daring or adventurous than the four of us girls. I think it was due to the fact they themselves had older sisters who paved the way for some of their "wilder" or more daring behavior.

Sometimes we would jump off the roof of our cousins' garage or sometimes off the roof of a friend's shed. (I look back and marvel none of us ever wound up with a broken ankle or foot.) I truly loved climbing trees—I didn't care if I WAS a girl! We sometimes even played on the lawns of people who were gone during the day at work. There was one lawn we particularly liked to play on. It was always well-manicured, though we never saw anyone ever working on it or even the people who lived there. Sometimes we crawled around and hid under the evergreen trees beneath the tree's branches which swept low to the ground. At times we even rolled down the sloping lawn that led out to the sidewalk.

I remember one time our mother instructed our babysitter to give us a "switching" if the babysitter ever found out we had gone to "Palisades Park," the ravine behind the house where we lived. (Our cousins, The Twins, had given the ravine its name.) At Palisades Park, we would slide down a narrow sandy path on a hillside, and that was about all we did. It wasn't very exciting at the "park", and there was lots of brush on both sides of the path to hinder investigating the ravine further. Our mother worried a lot about us playing there; I'm not sure why.

A day came when we disobeyed our mom and went to Palisades Park. (Later in life I learned there truly was a place called Palisades Park, but this ravine was not it!) Afterward, we must have confessed our misdeed to our babysitter—I do not know why—unless perhaps our consciences had been pricked. Our babysitter marched us outside onto the lawn and had all four of us sisters line up in a row. She then proceeded to break off a fresh twig from a nearby tree and "switch" our legs. Tears flowed freely down her face, but I don't recall any of us girls crying. I realized then that her punishment toward us had hurt her more than us, and my heart went out to her. Her tears caused me not to want to disobey my mother's rule again, and I don't recall ever going to Palisades Park again after that.

I remember one spring when little baby frogs crawled up from the ravine behind the house where we lived. They covered the backyard. I marveled at their plenteousness. They were a sight to behold! I also noticed moths and other insects flying around the outside porch light at night. Insects and amphibians caught my attention at a very early age. I felt a sense of closeness to God whenever I observed His creation in all its variety and freshness.

Later, my mother moved us to a place called "The Projects" where the poor people in our city could live cheaply. The Projects were actually quite nice, and the buildings were fairly new. Some of the families that lived there were couples with children, and others were single parents or divorcees like my mother raising children on their own. There were elderly couples who lived there too. Behind The Projects was a large field where wildflowers grew, and bees and butterflies came to feed on them.

And beyond this field was another ravine! My sisters and I loved to explore this ravine. It was huge, with lots of trees and a creek and interesting things to investigate. We were older now, and our cousins lived too far away for us to visit very often, so we found other playmates to interact with in our neighborhood.

One day the four of us went wading in the creek in the ravine with our little friend Mattie. Mattie was a black girl and we four were white. Suddenly Mattie started screaming and jumping up and down and yelling "Mama! Mama! Mama!" I looked at her to see what was wrong and saw several black leeches clinging to her feet and legs. Mattie instantly took off running and screaming for her mother, and I ran after her. I grabbed a stick along the way and chased her up the hill from the ravine and down several blocks of our neighborhood street and then onto the bridge that spanned the creek in which just minutes before we had been wading.

Mattie stopped on the bridge and hopped from one foot to the other, still screaming "Mama! Mama! Mama!" I wasn't Mattie's mama, but I told her to be still anyway. She wouldn't settle down at first. It was all I could do to convince her to stop jumping. Finally, after she had calmed down a bit, I was able to scrape the leeches off her legs and feet one by one with the stick I had snatched up earlier. It was a job getting them off, as their sucker-like mouths didn't want to let go. I don't remember what I did with their bodies, but I probably left them to shrivel up on the hot paved sidewalk of the bridge.

After the last leech was off her, Mattie finally calmed down. I sure was glad. I wasn't used to someone being so panic-stricken, and I knew it did her no good to behave like that. I was glad I had been able to help her, though she had been a challenge. I pondered why the leeches had gotten on her and not on us. It was either they were attracted to her darker skin or she had stepped in the wrong place in the creek or perhaps the rest of us had not gotten into the water and had crossed the creek via the stones in the creek. My recollection is fuzzy on that.

Anyway, when I look back on the incident, I realize, even at that young age, I was a "Miss Fix-It" or a "Miss Helper" or a "Helpful Henry". And to this day, even though I can't always fix it and I can't always help, I still try.

Taking the Cake

Andrea Foster

I screamed, "Noooooo!"

The cat went scooting across the floor after the dog, yowling as she went, knocking the table. I saw the cake begin to topple as if in slow motion. Danged critters!

I hadn't yet inserted the toothpicks, and the thing was still warm and wobbly, as it was. This was a dicey effort on my part, to begin with, but I needed to get it done, if I wanted to please my son Des and support the school bake sale. I've never been much of a baker—or a cook at that—but this was so important to Des.

And yet...splat! I saw it breaking into pieces as it fell, steaming as it went, and in a flash, the animals were racing back to gulp what they could of the sugary soft mountain that had hit the floor.

Buster dug in wholeheartedly. Kiki turned up her nose at the cake but tentatively licked the icing and liking the texture, gave it a go.

My heart sank, and I didn't even bother to yell at Buster and Kiki to stop. I too slid to the floor in a mound, just like the cake, crying steamy tears and wiping strands of hair out of my eyes, smudging icing on my chin, spreading crumbs across my lap.

Buster, hearing my distress, came over and put his big black squid lips in my face and offered a questioning albeit happy look on his little doggie face. He made a moaning sound that sounded like "Moooowmmy...".

Meanwhile, Kiki came over and began to do the full body cat rub and purr, satisfied with just a lick or two.
I wiped my tears, and Buster licked the swipe of icing on my cheek. Oh, goldarn it! I had to laugh. You knuckleheads, I thought.

At this point, my son Des came into the room, saying, "Whaaat???" and seeing the three musketeers commiserating on the kitchen floor, began to giggle. Phew!

The next day, we went out and bought the biggest pre-made box cake we could find at the local grocery store, and then we came home and used squeeze icing to decorate it before the sale—with, what else?—stick pictures of Buster and Kiki.

It sold out right away. Des was proud.

Tubs and the Train

Randel Conner

The intersection of Elm Street, where we crossed over into "the poor side of town", where we lived, was the scene of one of the most frightening experiences of my life. The incident happened one afternoon as I and my friends made our way home from the Saturday matinee at the Centre Theater, which had, by that time, replaced the old Rocket.

There were two sets of train tracks running parallel to each other. A second set of tracks were separated from the first set by about fifteen feet and were about five feet lower in elevation than the first set. This unusual configuration made it possible to actually jump the second set of tracks in a car at fifty miles per hour. Occasionally, we would encounter an inbound freight train threatening to block our passage to the next set of tracks.

When we saw a train approaching the Elm Street crossing, we took off running at record breaking speeds, except for Tubs, who couldn't run as fast as the rest of us. You could take it to the bank that Tubs would be the last person to cross in front of an oncoming train!

On this particular day, we were at least half a block away from the tracks when we saw an inbound freight train coming. The seven of us took off like a duck after a

June bug, in order to cross the tracks before the train could block us from the park. The problem was that Tubs was at least 500 feet behind us when we crossed the first set of tracks. We could all see that he wouldn't make it in time to beat the train.

We started screaming and motioning with our hands to stop, but Tubs, in a state of frenzy, just kept on coming. As he got closer and closer to the tracks, a sickening feeling came over me. I could see the end results of his pursuit. Unable to stop him, we watched in horror, (between the fingers of our hands that were covering our faces) as a solid blast of the train whistle screamed in our ears.

The engineer was waving his hands like windmill blades spinning out of control. Just as Tubs crossed the tracks, with the solid blast of the train whistle screaming in our ears, the front cow catcher of the train knocked the heel of his shoe into the air, like it was a piece of paper blowing in the wind. We all fell to the ground in dis-belief! Tubs was out of breath and as white as a sheet. We began to scream at him at the top of our lungs, telling him how stupid he was.

After we settled down, we had to help Tubs find his heel, so he would not have to explain to his mother what had happened. From that day forward, Tubs hated crossing anything that resembled railroad tracks, even in his mother's car.

When the kids in town found out about Tubs, he became a local celebrity. This was big news in Round Rock, and even a local reporter interviewed him and put his picture on the front page of the paper. The headlines read, "Local boy stares death in the face."

This story was on the lips of all the old men who met at the local coffee shop for some time to come.

Miss Angela's House

Hart Tillett

The blast seemed to shake the very foundations of the building for my chair gave a decided wobble. Doors and windows rattled. I grabbed the handle of my seat for support and assurance. A baby lying on her mother's lap screamed and was quickly hoisted to her breast to be cooed into quiescence. The Booom! Booom! Crack! Crack! Ear-splitting rumble had come in rapid, trailing succession, the echoes fading into the silence of the ethos.

A discharge like that could only be caused by large weaponry and with the uncontrolled gunrunning everywhere; the idea of terrorism was on everyone's mind, gauging by the frantic looks on their faces. I remember the brief dimming of the lights just before the bangs were heard, but like everyone else, I didn't think of lightning, believing instead that it was only the event manager's way to let the patrons know that the ceremonies were about to begin.

The occasion was the graduation ceremony for the Class of '77 of the Saint Cassian's Teachers Academy in Belize City. According to the program, there were eighteen graduates made up of fourteen young women and four men. Founded ten years before by an enterprising

Guyanese named Jeremy Pinkerton, Saint Cassian's was one of the most highly regarded teacher training educational institutions in the country. The raised platform of the Bliss Institute was adorned with jardinières of hibiscus, ti and bougainvillea. I looked at the program again. The ceremonies would start in less than a minute.

The pianist entered from the wings and settled herself at the Grand. At 6:00 o'clock exactly, she ran the first chords of *Here I Am Lord*, the school's song. The staff then entered and took their seats in the front row, each one gowned according to academic status. Once they were seated, there was another commotion as Dr. Pinkerton and the five-man Board of Management shuffled forwards, climbed the four stairs to the stage and found their seats.

The pianist waited till the last one had sat down, then began Elgar's famous graduation march, *Pomp and Circumstance*. All eyes turned to see the graduates coming into view through the wide doorway at the back. My friend Neely, whose full name appeared on the program as Cornelius Livingston Caliz, was the fourth to enter. As he neared where I sat, our eyes met, and I arched an eyebrow as a silent tribute to his achievement.

He was married and a father of two. It had to be tough ride for him. His childhood had been a challenge too. I remember the first time he talked about Miss Angela's house. There were five of us at a window table of the Pier Pointe Bar on the south bank of the Belize

River. There were Ramón Gallego and Tony Moss, who both worked at the Main Street Bank, Percy Rabon and myself, who were teachers at Padslowe High School, and Neely. All of us except him were graduates of St Cassian's.

"I was only eight years old," he had said then, "when I got to know Miss Angela."

"Who is Miss Angela?" asked Gallego, sipping loudly from his glass of rum-and-coke.

"Man," he replied, "you should have known her." He said this with a wistfulness that made us all look at him more closely. "I came from a large family. I was the ninth and last child of my parents." Large families are not unusual in British Honduras, so we left the statement up in the air to go where it would.

"My dad was a cruel man," he continued, "...to all of us, including my sisters and my mom. Mostly me, though, and I kept asking myself why. I stuttered badly as a child which I believe had a lot to do with it. All my mom would say when I asked her why he seemed to hate me, was that he did not hate me but was under a lot of pressure to care and feed us all. 'He doesn't seem to have problems when he's with his friends on weekends drinking,' I would say to her. 'He should stop drinking so much and maybe his problems would go away,' I urged in my childish wisdom."

"What happened, then?" I had asked.

"It was right after my eighth birthday, and my dad beat me severely for wetting my bed. The belt left long welts on my leg and the salve that Ma put on it didn't help."

It wasn't really an answer to my question, but I decided not to press the matter. He pulled on his cigarette, blew the smoke in perfect rings towards the ceiling before going on.

"I ran away!" He said it as if it was the most natural thing for a eight-year-old to do.

A lady who sold garnaches at the club approached our table and asked if we wanted any. Percy did an eye tally of the table and bought one each.

"Good boca," grunted Moss, examining the remnant held between thumb and forefinger. Garnaches are strictly finger food in Belize, even though it's best served hot.

The baby beside me broke into my reverie with a prolonged gurgle. The last of the graduates had taken their seats, and the music died. The MC for the occasion, was a Dr. Roger Wright from the Ministry of Education, according to the program. He now stepped up to the podium and looked officiously about the hall as if he expected an applause for just being there. Not getting any, he adjusted his glasses and said, "Ladies and gentlemen, will you please rise for the playing of the national anthem."

Like many others, including two dignitaries on the stage, I had to open the program to follow the words as the song was still not well-known. When it finally ended and we were again seated, Dr. Wright made a cursory look around the auditorium before beginning the introductions.

"Dr. Jeremy Pinkerton, Principal of St. Cassian's Teachers Academy," to which the principal gave a grave, humorless nod, appropriate for the occasion; "Dr. Fitzroy Barelydon, adjutant general of the Belize Defense Reservist and Grand Master of the Grand Masonic Lodge," who nodding stiffly; "Mr. Neil Hogstitt, President of...."

There followed the tiresome listing all the academic, social and economic standings of the dignitaries on stage. In the middle of one particularly long accolade, thunder struck again, though not as loud as before, but loud enough to make the MC lay his script down and smile wryly until quiet returned.

I glanced at the program and was surprised to see that the cleric chosen to offer the blessing was John MacDonald, S.J., a young priest from the St Paul's parish, whose sermons, heavily seasoned with a tincture of social justice, had made him an instant household name far beyond his parish. The MC was finishing his welcoming speech.

"And now," he said, turning to Father John and nodding slightly, "we have the honor..." *Has he ever had to sit through boring introductions?* I asked myself. The priest went to the podium.

"Let us pray," he began. *My kind of speaker*, I thought. The prayer was short but it had everything. His eloquent voice enthralled us, and because of that, I almost missed what had to be the most important part of the prayer. "Guide the hearts and minds of these your servants," he intoned, "who will now go back to their classrooms to use the training they received at St. Cassian's, to teach their pupils the greatest lesson of their lives, which is that they love one another, whether rich or poor, blessed with good understanding or not so fortunate, from the Northside...." I looked up then to see how the words affected Neely, for I was recalling his reason for running away from home. His head was bowed prayerfully.

"Where did you go?" Rabon had asked him. "Family?" he ventured.

"No," he had said, somewhat embarrassed. "I had a friend from my class named Codrington, we all called him Caddie, who used to take me to his mom's after school, on days when we had a lot of homework to do. I had told him how hard it was for me to get my assignments done, once Daddy got home from work."

"Miss Angela?" prompted Gallego, licking the last bit of his garnaches.

"Yes, the sweetest lady I've ever known."

We all frowned, playfully of course, at which he admitted, "After my mom, of course."

Another round of drinks was ordered, and while we waited, Percy kept the topic warm by asking him about his parents' reaction.

"I think they were both glad that I'd left," he said despairingly. "My dad, because he didn't have to see me every day and my mom, because there was no more beating for her to witness." He twirled his empty glass meditatively, then said: "You wouldn't believe what he said to me once. 'Boy,' he always called me that, 'I spoke with God after you were born, and you know what He said? He said he thought He had made a mistake.' My dad had a devilish way to smile when he thought he'd said something that was painful and funny. He gave me that smile then, then added, 'And you know what I told Him? I told Him that He was right!'"

The jukebox suddenly came to life as Charlie Pride began the first strains of *Ka Liga*. We all hummed along until the chorus and then joined Charlie with:

"Poor old Ka Liga

He never got a kiss…"

Neely was talking again. "You know something," he said, "I don't remember my father ever kissing or hugging me, know what I mean? Not the kind that the Indian missed out on, but the affectionate, playful hug of a father embracing a son. I have two kids now, and I hug them all the time."

The waitress brought the drinks, was paid and went to serve another table. We raised our drinks in a toast and drank.

"It's like he didn't want to touch me, or even be near to me. 'Ma protested this treatment at first, but there was no change in his attitude towards me. 'He's your child,' she used to tell him. 'Why can't you act like a father to him?' After a while, she just stopped, out of despair or anger or something. I dunno...."

It was the unmistakable *huic... huic...* sounds coming from of the baby that brought me back to the graduation ceremony.

"Ladies and gentlemen," the MC was saying, "we will now take time out to recognize the individual performances of some of our students." My interest, as a past awardee, was the Principal's Prize, bestowed on the student with the highest scores for the two-year course duration in three core subjects: Child Psychology, Sociology and The Teaching Craft. Additional credits were considered for leadership, creativity and all-round compatibility.

"I am pleased to announce that the prize for Best Sportsman of the year," said the MC, in a voice that was not half as pleasant as it was formal. "This individual has shown…" *Who cares about athletics that much,* I asked myself. It wouldn't be Neely, short, wiry and studious as he was. Neely!

When he had said "dunno" that afternoon, after blaming his father for not showing him any affection, Moss had asked the question that all of us wanted to know: "How long did you stay at Miss Angela's?"

"Stay?" He was incredulous. "I never went back home."

"But they must've sent messages to her?" he pressed.

"Not that I knew of," he countered. "She would've told me."

There was a pause. Neely seemed to be weighing his mind. Finally, he continued.

"You see, Miss Angela was a different person from my parents. She listened. To her, you were the only person in the house. If we had a problem, she didn't mind leaving whatever she was doing to help us work it out. If it was personal, she would take us out on the verandah, the only private place in that full house, and talk about it."

"You keep saying 'Us,'" observed Ramon, lighting up a cigarette. "How many children did they have?"

"None." Looks of confusion suddenly made him explain. "None of their own, I mean. You see, Miss Angela lost her first child during childbirth and was never able to have another after that. Something to do with an infection and an operation."

"So," continued Ramon, musingly, "none of the children there were hers?"

"None!" He said it flatly, but we could feel the pride one hears when a child brags about his parents.

"Who were they, then?" quizzed Percy, smacking his lips after a deep draught of his beer. "And how did they end up with her?"

Little baby by my side was now relaxed and blew air from partly opened lips; I was back from the Pier Pointe Bar and into the unfolding events on the stage, having missed out on all but the last award.

"And now," purred the MC, fussing unnecessarily with his tie, "we come to that moment that all the students are waiting for, the awardee of the Principal's Prize. This year it goes to a student who, for the past two years has maintained straight A's, not only in the stipulated three core subjects, but has done so in four of the other five subjects in the curriculum. Besides that, we were impressed by the way that student had mobilized the student body to reach out during last Christmas season, to help underprivileged children in this neighborhood have a better Christmas. Gifts solicited from businesses were wrapped at the school after classes; cards were addressed personally to the children." He mopped perspiration from his face and neck, and sipped from the bottle of water that sat on the ledge of the podium. "At times," he chuckled, "the classrooms looked more like Santa's workshop."

"Ladies and gentlemen, on behalf of the Principal, Staff and the graduates, I am pleased to announce that this year's winner of the Principal's Prize is Mr. Cornelius Caliz." The room erupted in clapping. Neely rose to accept the applause and made his way to the podium. At the same time, Dr. Pinkerton got up and went to join him and the MC.

"Please accept this as a token of the school's deep appreciation for the good example you have shown to the student body over these past two years." He gave Neely a gift-wrapped package, and as both the principal and the MC left the podium, Neely stepped forward to say his thanks. The baby sneezed twice, and my attention turned instead to what Neely had told us about his gratitude to Miss Angela.

"When she took me in, there were already seven

kids under her roof. Man, I tell you, bunk beds were the order of the day. There just wasn't any place for me and for the first two months, I had to sleep on the dining room floor. You might think that that was hard, but I loved it. Her kitchen always had a smell of food, and I went to sleep many-a-night thinking of breakfast." He was smiling as he shared this tidbit.

"Did you ever get up after everyone was asleep to…?

He didn't let Peter finish the question. "No way. She trusted us and we worshipped her. There was nothing we'd do to hurt her feelings."

"Did you ever get your own bed?" asked Percy.

He ran his hand through his hair that kept tumbling over his forehead. "Oh yes," he said. "Miss Angela had Mr. Cecil, her husband, add a little room to the baking room at the back. It became my room until she realized there was space for one more 'child.'"

"I can see why you adore her so," said Ramon. "What else did she do?"

"Yeah! A thousand things, man. The thing I liked her for most, though, was the way she helped me overcome my stuttering. Pa couldn't stand it when my answers took too long."

"Hard to tell now that you ever did," I put in.

"All thanks to Miss Angela, Nathan," he explained. "She didn't allow the others who, at first, laughed at me. Miss Angela—did I tell you she is a black lady? Well, that ebony face sure must've turned red, though we couldn't see it, the first time one of them laughed. She didn't get up. She didn't raise her voice. She just looked at the culprit and hissed: 'Don't you ever, ever let me catch you doing that again!' she had said. And that was that. There was no more teasing."

"One more thing." His voice had taken on a pleading tone as if to say that what he would tell us next was to be taken as gospel. "Although amongst the eight of us, there were three schools that she had to deal with, she never missed a Parent Teachers' meeting at any of them. When a teacher would send a note home, whatever the reason, she would walk to the school to deal personally with whatever the matter was. She was our mother, and we were her kids, man, and that made her push for us. How could we, her Indian, Garifuna, Spanish and Creole 'children' not love her?"

It was the baby again, and this time its mother discreetly suckled it, the chugging sound bringing me back to the program. Just in time, too, to hear the MC's introduction of the valedictorian. Neely had told me about it, and that was the main reason for my presence there. I silently hoped that his speech handicap would not intrude because of the excitement.

"…and I now present to you the valedictorian for the 1977 graduation class of St. Cassian's Teachers Academy. Ladies and gentlemen, please join me in welcoming to the podium once more, Mr. Cornelius Caliz."

He went through his speech saying the usual things about assignments, students' aspirations, challenges injuggling work and studies and so on. Then he came to the part about family support. He had told us before, that within four years after he had run away, his parents had gone to America and not come back. It was not until his father had died, that his mother had returned home for a visit, and he, by that time a married man with a family of his own, was finally able to have her meet Miss Angela. Naturally, at this reference to family, I sat upright for what would follow.

He thanked his absent mother without whom, he said, grinning, he would not be on the platform that night. He praised her for the fond memories of his early childhood, given in spite of his dad's cruelties.

"But the person who has brought me through the rigors of later childhood, and who guided me, and was there to answer those questions that trouble us all in our incipient teen years, that person is my second Mom, Mrs. Angela F-f-flowers who everyone knows as Miss Angela."

Oh my, I said to myself, *slow down, Neely.*

That was one of the lessons that Miss Angela had taught him to help overcome his stutter. It was Percy who had picked up the conversation about his stammering, that I had started.

"And how did she help?" he had asked.

"There were three things she kept saying when the stammering started: talk more slowly, breathe deeply and lengthen the letters that gave problems. So I would say 'br-r-ead' or 't-ee-e-cher', and it worked. She had me breathe slowly and deeply as I said those letters that gave me the most problems. And always with the greatest of patience."

Moss twirled the ice cubes about in his glass. "There's something I always wanted to ask. Where did she get the money to feed you all? You were kids so you couldn't pay her for it...?

"Everyone knew and liked Miss Angela. Mr. Chin, the Chinaman that owned the neighborhood bakery, set aside five loaves for her every other day. And Mrs. Miley, the butcher's wife? Well she made sure that he reserved a bit of liver, or a piece of shank every Thursday for us. Another provided her with 'belly fat', that butchers call the 'plate,' on Tuesdays." He drew on his cigarette and then added. "Each of us who collected the bread, the meat and other donations, had to be introduced personally by her to the donors. I remember when it was my turn to start. The butcher looked from her to me and said, 'Neely, here's some plate for your next plate!' He guffawed and I liked him instantly."

The baby was making flat tire sounds with its lips, and I looked up at the stage in time to see Neely step back from the podium briefly as he acknowledged the cheering. We all thought he had finished, but then he hugged the lectern again. The handclaps stopped as if on cue.

"What do most children remember about their mother?" he asked. "The bedtime stories? The gentle hugs? The cooking and the ironing? The encouragement when things weren't going right?" He paused to get the audience on board with him once more.

"Why," he began rhetorically, "they remember all of those moments. I do! Miss Angela permeated her house with an abundance of such care. What made her special was the depth of feeling that haloed her eyes. For anyone can hug you, read for you, or just do for you. Anyone, but not her. Through her gentle comforting, solicitous eyes, she asked us to accept the hug, the story, the care, as gifts from her." He had paused again, surveying the audience.

"I have done my best tonight to paint a picture of her, hoping that I have been able to have planted a desire in your hearts to get to know her. Well," he said conversationally, "she is with us, and at this time I'll ask her to stand."

There was a slight commotion in the front row. Seconds passed. Necks craned. Finally, the woman made it up with the help of the man who sat beside her. She leaned lightly on her cane. Miss Angela was an amputee; had been so since the 1931 hurricane that robbed her of her left leg! There were gasps across the auditorium. Cameras flashed.

Then the applause began. It lasted for perhaps a minute during which handkerchiefs were produced.

Everybody was standing as Neely left the stage to go and embrace her. The remainder of the program—the presentation of the candidates, the conferral of diplomas, closing remarks and the recessional—all went by with the haste of an anticlimactic finish.

The following day, the papers carried the story with headlines like, *Miss Angela's House for Lost Kids* and *Miss Angela Brought the House Down*! The one I liked the best was *Mother of the Year Unveiled*!

An Unbelievable Coincidence

Rosemarie Durgin

It was on a Friday afternoon that my friend Cecile called to invite me to join her and a few friends for drinks at the little Mexican restaurant and bar after work. I was baby-sitting the local branch of the Savings and Loan institution; I was working for that day. Cecile was working at the branch office of the S&L, across the street from where I was that day.

Cecile and I had met while attending classes of the Institute for Financial Education offered through the Savings and Loan Associations. The classes were offered and paid for by our organizations and held in the offices of the various S&Ls and taught by their officers. We were both in the same situation; both recently divorced from prominent mates and struggling with advancing our careers, children and our households. Cecile had been married to a psychiatrist, and I to a radio news director. We often studied together over the phone on weekends and after class. We had become fast friends very quickly.

So, on that particular day, my children all had places they had to be, and I was free to enjoy a margarita or two. After work, I drove the half- block to the restaurant across the parking lots and joined Cecile and her friends in the bar of the little restaurant.

They were all seated around a table, and when my friend saw me, she called out, "Rose, come on over here, have a seat." After introductions were made, the conversations swirled around me. By my second margarita, I was totally engaged in conversation with my table neighbors, not paying much attention to my friend. That is, until she uttered one word. I have no idea what brought the conversation to that word, but the word was "Bamberg." That caught my attention.

I completely ignored the conversation with my tablemates and asked Cecile across the table, "What do you know about Bamberg?"

"Quite a lot, I lived there when I was little. Why?"

"When?"

"From 1947 to 1951. Why?"

"I lived there too, from 1945 to the end of summer 1948."

"No!"

"Where did you live in Bamberg, at the old Caserne, the military barracks?"

"No, we lived in town near the Bahnhof, the train station. It was a big wide avenue, in a big old house, with lots of other families. I can't pronounce the name of the street, Lup… something."

All sorts of memories passed through my mind as she said this. It was eerie. I was back there again in Germany.

"You lived in the old hotel, the Bamberger Hof, a grand old hotel with steps going down to the sidewalk and a red carpet on them, on Luitpoldstrasse at the corner with Heiliggrabstrasse. There was a huge chandelier in the foyer and a liveried doorman."

"Yeah, that's it. How did you know that?"

"I lived just down the street from you at Heiliggrabstrasse number 40. I went past your house every day on my way to school and back home again. I went to Luitpold School, about two blocks away from your house, towards the river, on the other side of the street."

"No," she breathed and everyone at the table had become quiet; all conversation had stopped as they watched us open mouthed.

I continued, "Every morning, just about the time my friends and I passed the old hotel, a car would leave the garages of the hotel, which were in the back of the building and emptied into Heiliggrabstrasse, full with American children on their way to school. We all hated those cars, for they were so quiet, we had trouble hearing them over the noise of the old Mercedes and Opels on the road. We had to cross that busy street and had been surprised a few times by the approach of those vehicles.

We called those cars 'Scheicher', creepers, sneakers."

"Oh, my God, Rose, I was one of the children in that staff car on our way to school. I can't believe you were one of those kids we were so envious of. We hated that smelly, old car, we had to sit still in, and we were not allowed to talk. You guys would laugh and run or skip and play on the way to school. Wow, that is really something."

"And I was envious of you. You were driven to school. We had to walk in all kinds of weather, in rain or shine, in cold or snow. It was not so much fun. And we had to carry our heavy satchels, with our slate tablets and books. Those slate tablets were heavy and broke easy, and were expensive. My mother would have had trouble buying me another, if I had damaged it. Oh, the boys did not admit they were envious too. They were too big, too manly for that, but we girls would gladly have changed places with you. I remember there was one little dark-haired girl that would always turn around. She sat in the middle of the back seat and waved at us."

"That little girl was me! I always got in trouble for waving at all of you. I remember, there were usually three girls that walked in that group, two little ones, and one girl with long dark braids who was a bit taller than the others and so very skinny. She always waved back at me."

"That was me. I always waved back."

"But you are short now, just like me. That girl was

taller than her companions."

"Yea, me. I was almost two years older than the others, because I could not start school when I should have. There were none then. And I was tall then. I have not grown a hair since before my twelfth birthday. I was 154 cm then, and I am still 5'2" today. I was so envious of your ponytail. I was not allowed to wear my hair that way, not German enough. Those long braids took forever in the mornings to braid."

"And I thought they were so cool."

Everyone at the table found it a fascinating and an unbelievable coincidence that we had been aware of each other thirty-five years ago, in another country, and now had finally made the connection, although we had been friends for two years already. Cecile and I remained friends and talked often about our time in Bamberg, until life took us in different directions.

The Fields Were my Friends

Andrea Foster

The fields were my friends. We did everything there, flew kites, played baseball, chased cows until the bull chased us away, and I knew every blade of grass, every pathway, every boulder and snake in the stone fence that corralled the fields.

The fields were my dream home. We rolled in the grass to bend it down and made rooms, apartments, mansions filled with mice and ants and lady bug residents, in addition to us, the playful giants.

The fields were sports arenas, where we mowed and fashioned real fields of dreams, where my brother sat on first base, waiting for a play to happen. And the kids did come to our neighborhood baseball field, old and young alike, some sitting on the nearby boulder fences like bleachers and cheering for family members to make the perfect play.

The fields were a maze for meditation, where I walked our bull-mastiff Biff in silence and contemplation, the two of us allowing our imaginations to fly and our senses to vibrate to the gentlest of frequencies.

In winter, the fields became an icy mountain that sloped down to a pond, and we would ride our brightly-colored wooden bobsled down to the icy saucer, feeling like Olympic athletes on a luge run.

In spring and summer, the fields offered wild-flowers and chestnut-colored horses chewing wooden fences. I knew all their names, both the flowers and the horses.

In fall, I collected the rainbow-colored leaves from the trees that edged the fields and pressed them between wax paper with an iron, the smell musty and hot and good.

The fields beat a path to the orchard nearby, where we'd collect dropped fruit for pies and chew abandoned grapes, chewy with soft centers, staining our lips dark.

At the central hub of the fields stood a giant oak tree that we pretended was a seedling of the famed Charter Oak that had hidden the state's constitution in revolutionary times. In my mind, I can still see the size and shape of its leaves and vividly imagine its shade where we played many a day. Although my mother once saved that colossal tree from the developers with pleas and signatures, if you look on Google Earth now, there looks to be a black hole where it once grew, that holy place that had been the center of my childhood universe.

Every marvel of nature lived there in those fields and intrigued me and drew a web around me that will forever in my mind be a place of peace, joy, wonder, and fascination.

Thank you, Momma Ceres, and all your critter-children, for a playground far more beautiful—and fun—than a swing set or a slide.

Be Kind, and Don't Hang Out with Jerks

Julianna Kubilis

My life right now is so interesting. I'm in kindergarten, and I love school. I love everything about school, except for waking up early and having to find the motivation to get to school. On this sunny morning, I walk out the front door to find my mom in the driver's seat of our baby blue Plymouth Horizon, waiting on me as usual. My little sister is in the back seat, oblivious to everything, except for the way her thumb fits so perfectly in her two-year-old mouth. I hurry down the steps of our trailer and trot my way to the car to hop in the back seat and quickly shut the door. My mom looks at me in the rearview mirror with one eyebrow raised, telling me without words, that I need to get my act together in the mornings, because she is sick of my snail's pace of getting ready for school. I can read her eyebrows even better than I can read my Berenstain Bears books. The things my mom's eyebrows can say would blow your mind.

I really love this blue car. My grandpa bought the car for my mom, from my grandma's parents, because they didn't want the car anymore. I don't know why they didn't want this car anymore, it is so glorious. The car is just as blue as the sky, and the view out the huge rear window is amazing. I love watching the people behind us driving
their cars, talking with each other, waving at me with their

big finger (whatever that means), and flick little things out of their windows. Riding in this car is fun.

Our car backs down our short driveway into the street they call Longfellow. We stop, and then back up some more. We stop again, and my mom starts pulling at the metal stick that is by her leg, as hard as she can, slapping it, telling the stick that this was not funny. Why is she talking to the stick that moves the car? Why are we not going? I look out the back window to see if anything is going to run into us. Thankfully, the street is clear as far away as I can see. The streets in our trailer park are nice and straight and hardly ever busy. Cats feel free to walk them lazily, and kids feel safe to cross them without looking.

The metal stick is still not moving. The button on the stick is going in, but even though my mom is using both her hands to pull the stick towards her, the stick will not move.

"Screw it," she says, as she throws her right arm around the seat next to her, shimmies her hips in her seat and stares out the back of the car through that big window and hits the gas.

I can feel my eyes get big as my body is flung forward. My mom is driving our blue car backwards, very quickly.

"I guess this is just how you're getting to school now. In reverse. How fun!"

My mom smiles, but she doesn't seem as happy as she usually does when she's smiling. My sister, sucking her pruney thumb, looks at me with her big brown eyes, and those eyes of hers are filled with questions. Questions like, "What are we doing?" and "Why is everything in front of me getting smaller?" and "Why does my thumb taste so good?"

We whip around a corner; my mom's face looks worried for a split second, but then out of nowhere, she is immediately brave again, like she has just done something that was hard, really well. I guess making the corner without running into someone's car or through someone's yard is quite the accomplishment. Yay, mom! She is proud of herself at this point; her eyes are squinting, her teeth biting at the corner of her lip, her one eyebrow arched as if she knows something that we don't.

My mom drives us backwards through the trailer park, all the way to where the trailer park road meets the main road they called Ten Mile. Ten Mile is a real road, with real people and real cars that run over the real cats who are trying to cross the street. Kids do not walk down this road. This is a serious road, and driving down this road backwards is going to take some serious skill. My mom has tons of skills, and driving a little car in reverse is one of them. She only has to go a couple of blocks down Ten Mile to get me to my school. My mom can do that, because my mom can do anything. My mom waits for a second at the stop sign and then makes her move.

We pull onto Ten Mile, rear end first. We aren't on Ten Mile for more than a couple of seconds before someone honks at us. I look around to see who is honking, but can't find them. I decide that the best course of action is just to wave at everyone, that way they won't have to honk to get my attention. I start waving to the guys in the truck that I can see in front of me, and I wave at the old lady I see next to me. My sister starts waving too, mainly to my mom, but I think my mom really appreciates that we are being so polite.

"Thank goodness we live so close."

My mom is looking a little nervous. Does she not like driving this way? Going backwards the whole way to school has been quite fun for my sister and me. Surely this is an adventure for her too. The closer we get to my elementary school, the more relaxed my mom's face is. Instead of dropping me off by the door, she pulls into a parking space.

"Please, God, just make this stupid thing go forward!"

My mom puts both hands on the stick with the button, grunts, and then roars like a baby lion, and the stick goes forward!

"Yes! Yes! We did it! Oh my word, I can't believe we did it!"

My mom is so happy. She puts her hands up in the air, wiggles her butt in her seat and plays the drums on the thin, blue steering wheel. My little sister even pulls her thumb out of her mouth to cheer for my mom's victory. Our celebration lasts just for a moment before I am re-minded that I have to go off to school.

"Get out, get your stuff. We need to get in there, so I can call your grandpa and tell him what a fun morning we had."

I knew she had liked driving backwards! Who

wouldn't?

As we walk through the big glass doors of my school, my mom puts her hand on my head and tells me the same thing that she has told me every other morning before I go off to school.

"I love you. Have a good day. Be kind, and don't hang out with jerks."

My day has started out very backwards, but my mom single handedly has spun my day around, and I am now back on track, heading in the right direction. That is what mothers do; they take the crazy in life, and they make it seem fun and normal.

Happy Mother's Day!

Be kind, and don't hang out with jerks!

About the Authors

PJ Acker is an artist and writer with an eye out for the next adventure while living in the land of many tornados. She loves writing, painting, kayaking, biking and adventures and is a member of Romance Writers of America as well as Creative Quills. She lives with her husband and two pushy cats.

Kandy Anderson began writing at the young age of twelve years old. She recently began a series of children's books with her eight-year-old daughter in 2016. Her passion for working with young adults inspired her to start the company STEM4KIDS LLC, in hopes of introducing young girls to science and creative arts. She is a member of Creative Quills and the Society of Children's Book Writers & Illustrators. When not writing, Kandy likes to research natural cures for cancer and make up batches of homemade Kombucha Tea.

Chuck Baker is a retired businessman and widower living in Stroud, OK. Now a published author specializing in human interest short stories, both fact and fiction, many with an ironic ending. He is a member of both Creative Quills and Oklahoma Writers, Inc. His latest book of short stories is titled *Twisted Snapshots*.

Alicia Ballard is a student at Redlands Community College in El Reno, Oklahoma and an employee of the El Reno Carnegie Library. She actually was a member of our writing group before she joined the library staff! Alicia is also a gifted horror writer.

Judy K. Bishop writes inspirational children's books, poetry, short stories and essays. She currently has a book of poetry available called *Poetry Pathways*. Before becoming a member of Oklahoma Writers, Inc., Romance Writers of America, and Creative Quills, she previously lived in Hawaii for almost twenty years. She currently resides in Choctaw, OK.

Glenda Brown is a writer with a wry sense of humor that shows in her short stories. She is a former social worker who lives with her husband Dan in Yukon, OK. She is currently writing a mystery titled *The Reading Tree.*

Karen Bullock comes from a long line of story tellers. All of her father's family could weave a story from the smallest incident. You were never sure if they were the truth, a slight exaggeration, or a down-right lie. It didn't matter; they were always entertaining and interesting. She has worked as an oil field laboratory technician and field chemist before entering a career as a science educator. After retiring, she has continued to work as a biology teacher at a local junior college. She is currently working on two books, an anthology of her family and life lessons learned by observing nature. Karen spends her free time reading, writing, walking her dog and training him to become a therapy dog. She recently won an award from the Rose State Writers Conference for a nostalgic poem she wrote.

Randel Conner, a farm boy from central OK, grew up in the small town of El Reno. At age 21, he published his first book *To Die is Gain* which was sold in Oklahoma, Texas and Arkansas. His next book was *America's Most Embarrassing Moments* which is still a work in progress. The story in this volume is from his current book titled *The Round Rock Seven.* He is a member of the Creative Quills in El Reno and has written articles for RV magazines and several religious papers.

Charlotte M. Cooper is a new member of Creative Quills Writing Group. She is new to writing and lives in El Reno, OK, with her husband and six kitties!

Alton "Tuna" Dobbins retired from the Air Force in 1996 with over 2000 hours in single seat attack jets. He then worked for the Federal Aviation Administration as a technical writer until retiring in 2015. Tuna is the author of two fiction novels: *Crossbow Revenge* and *Alice Was Not Her Name,* both action-packed murder mysteries, released respectively in 2016 and 2017. Tuna is a fan of fast cars and participates in shows and open road racing in his Corvette. He resides in Mustang, OK with his wife Susan.

Kaylene Dow grew up in the shadows of the Glass Mountains of Oklahoma. She devoted thirteen years to the banking industry prior to becoming an educator. Unsolved family mysteries fuel her passion for research and writing. She has discovered truth can be stranger than fiction, yet believes a few embellished details can't hurt. Kaylene is a member of ACFW and OCFW. She is currently working on a novel, *Where There's a Will.*

Rosemarie Durgin Aguilar was born just before WWII in Germany. She came to America in 1963 and is the mother of four and grandmother of ten. She is retired, except for writing full time! She currently has two books published, *Kinder Castle* and *Mail Order Bride*, with a third in the works! She is a member of Romance Writers of America. Besides writing, Rosemarie enjoys traveling, reading, needlework, wildlife and photography. Rosemarie lives with her husband John in Bethany, Oklahoma, with a menagerie of cats and dogs.

Clay Fees is a lifelong aficionado of American muscle cars from the 1960s and '70s, having owned a 1968 Plymouth Road Runner for his first car in the late 1980s. He is a 1991 graduate of Kellyville (OK) High School, and holds a Bachelor's of Arts degree from the University of Central Oklahoma, as well as a Juris

Doctorate and Master's degree in American History from the University of Tulsa. A former high school history teacher and baseball coach as well as college professor of American History, Clay is a veteran of the Global War on Terror having been deployed with the US Army to the Arab Republic of Egypt. Currently a full-time member and officer of the Oklahoma National Guard, he lives in Kellyville, where he spends time tinkering with his dad tinkering on old cars and attending car shows. His current literary project is a brief history of the muscle car era with a working title of *The Rise and Fall of the American Muscle Car.*

Debbie Fogle is a member of Creative Quills writers of El Reno, Oklahoma and a member of the Romance Writers of America / Oklahoma Chapter (OKRWA). She has her first indie novel, *Happiness is Hard to Find*, available on iUniverse.com and several short stories in collection publications. She was the IDA 2016 judge for OKRWA and the NRCA 2017 Coordinator for OKRWA. She shares her adventures in her writing and lives life to the fullest.

Andrea Foster is an editor and author who has been in the book business and has been editing since 1977. She currently teaches Writing and Composition at Redlands Community College, Creative Writing at the Carnegie Library in El Reno, and How to Write, Publish & Market Your Book at the Canadian Valley Technology Center, CVTech. She has been published in various magazines and newspapers and has a number of non-fiction books. She recently published her first Young Adult paranormal novel *Helena and the Haunted Hospital.* She currently resides in Kingfisher, OK.

Johnna Kaye is a graduate of the University of

Oklahoma, where she earned her master's degree in French literature. Before starting her family, she spent a year living in France and ten years teaching French in the United States. Author of *Token* and *Viral* of The Casdan Chronicles series, Kaye resides in central Oklahoma with a devoted husband, two teenage children, two cats, and one very pesky dog.

Julianna Kubilis is a wife, mother, full-time college student, and a lover of all things beautiful and Christ centered. She was raised in Michigan, but moved to Oklahoma in 2007. Julianna currently lives with her husband and three children in El Reno, Oklahoma.

Bernadette Lowe is a grandmother who loves writing stories for her granddaughter. She is currently working on a project to make legal forms and papers available to the public via her website http://www.landlordforms.us . She grew up on a dairy farm and lives in Oklahoma City, OK.

Julie Marquardt is a haiku poet extraordinaire and a young adult author. Her current book project, about to be published, named *Brigantina's Journey*, is about a sea-loving young lady from the 1800s who finds herself mixed up with pirates and other adventures. At the same time, she is awakening to the realization that she is quickly growing up and becoming a young lady, whether she wants to or not. Formerly a nurse, Julie currently resides in Oklahoma, and writes whenever she can. She has a short story published in *Alternate Perspectives* and *Tales and Trails: A Western Odyssey*. She is a member of Romance Writers of America. To learn more about Julie Marquardt and her projects, visit her webpage: www.wordsbyjulie.info.

Kevin McCarthy is a student of Keystone private on-line High School. He enjoys playing video games and attending DeMolay leadership conferences. *Home* is his first publication.

Carol Nichols worked in the legal profession since her junior year of high school as a legal secretary for an El Reno law firm. She worked for the Canadian County Sheriff's Office under four different administrations and with the District Attorney's Office. After a move to southern Illinois, she worked for a criminal defense attorney before moving to Pennsylvania. In Pennsylvania, Carol started writing through journals to deter loneliness caused by separation from family.

After returning to El Reno in 1992, she worked for USDA at Ft. Reno before retiring. Carol's journey continued with family illness and the death of her husband, Glen, thus heightening her awareness of life's fragility. Carol found release in writing and expresses her feelings about life, marriage and faith in her writings. Carol has published one mystery romance novel titled *A Different Season* and is working on her second, *Mists of the Moment.* She is a member of Romance Writers of America. She now resides in El Reno with her Jack Russell terrier, Patches.

Sue D. L. Smith is a gifted writer and editor with a strong philosophical flair and varied life experiences that manifest in her short stories and fiction. She recently graduated *summa cum* laude with an Associate in Arts from Redlands Community College. She has three published short stories with the writing group: "Harry the Lowly Worm," "The Cowboy from Hell," and "Legs and Leeches". Sue is a true Renaissance woman who enjoys painting and sketching, singing, and photographing nature. She lives in El Reno, Oklahoma, with her loving and supportive husband Bruce and their indoor and outdoor kitties, Miss Kitty, Yellow Kitty, and a new addition,

Oreo.

Connie Sweeney has retired recently from a thirty-five year banking career to focus on her next career – in writing. She has two grown sons, and lives on a ranch in Oklahoma with her husband, lots of cattle, wheat and big round bales of hay. She has written various short stories and has published her first children's book entitled *Oakie: A Tree and a Boy*. She is currently writing a children's book series about her two farm dogs, Newt and Bella.

Hart Tillett was born in British Honduras (Belize). He graduated from Carleton University (Canada) with an honors degree in Economics and thereafter devoted his professional life to banking and insurance. He plays cricket, enjoys horseback riding, is a chess enthusiast and open water scuba diver. His entry "Yoli" placed second in the NOSTALGIA category of the 2015 writing contest sponsored by the Oklahoma City Writers, Inc. His first novel, just released, is entitled *Exiles No More*, an historical novel set in Belize in the 1800s. Hart lives in Belize but resides for much of the year in Oklahoma City. He and his wife have four children.

Other Books by Creative Quills

Alternate Perspectives

Tales and Trails: A Western Odyssey

Upcoming Books by Creative Quills

Angst and Acne: Teenage Tales

Modern Day Myths

Halloween Horrors

Other Books by our authors:

(available on the Createspace store, Amazon, and Kindle)

Twisted Snapshots by Chuck Baker

Poetry Pathways by Judy K. Bishop

Alice is not Her Name by A. "Tuna" Dobbins

Crossbow Revenge by A. "Tuna" Dobbins

Kinder Castle by Rosemarie Durgin

Mail Order Bride by Rosemarie Durgin

Happiness is Hard to Find by Debbie Fogle

Helena and the Haunted Hospital by Andrea Foster

Brigantina's Journey by Julie Marquardt

A Different Season by Carol Nichols

Oakie: A Tree and a Boy by Connie Sweeney

Exiles No More by Hart Tillett

Websites:

http://www.creativequills.com
http://www.okwriters.com
http://www.writeok.com
http://www.renocity.us
http://www.meetup.com/CreativeQuills/
http://www.thebooklady.info

Thanks to all our beta-readers for proofing the book:
Rosemarie Durgin and her husband, Julie Marquardt
and her dad, Carol Nichols, and Sue D. L. Smith.

48724768R00115

Made in the USA
San Bernardino, CA
03 May 2017